The Curlytops At Uncle Frank's Farm

Howard Roger Garis

HE CURLYTOPS AT UNCLE FRANK'S RANCH

CHAPTER I

TROUBLE'S TUMBLE

"Say, Jan, this isn't any fun!"

"What do you want to play then, Ted?"

Janet Martin looked at her brother, who was dressed in one of his father's coats and hats while across his nose was a pair of spectacles much too large for him. Janet, wearing one of her mother's skirts, was sitting in a chair holding a doll.

"Well, I'm tired of playing doctor, Jan, and giving your make-believe sick doll bread pills. I want to do something else," and Teddy began taking off the coat, which was so long for him that it dragged on the ground.

"Oh, I know what we can do that'll be lots of fun!" cried Janet, getting up from the chair so quickly that she forgot about her doll, which fell to the floor with a crash that might have broken her head.

"Oh, my dear!" cried Janet, as she had often heard her mother call when Baby William tumbled and hurt himself. "Oh, are you hurt?" and Janet clasped the doll in her arms, and hugged it as though it were a real child.

"Is she busted?" Ted demanded, but he did not ask as a real doctor might inquire. In fact, he had stopped playing doctor.

"No, she isn't hurt, I guess," Jan answered, feeling of her doll's head. "I forgot all about her being in my lap. Oh, aren't you going to play any more, Ted?" she asked as she saw her brother toss the big coat on a chair and take off the spectacles.

"No. I want to do something else. This is no fun!"

"Well, let's make-believe you're sick and I can be a Red Cross nurse, like some of those we saw in the drugstore window down the street, making bandages for the soldiers. You could be a soldier, Ted, and I could be the nurse, and I'd make some sugar pills for you, if you don't like the rolled-up bread ones you gave my doll."

2

Teddy Martin thought this over for a few seconds. He seemed to like it. And then he shook his head.

"No," he answered his sister, "I couldn't be a soldier."

"Why not?"

"'Cause I haven't got a gun and there isn't any tent."

"We could make a tent with a sheet off the bed like we do lots of times. Put it over a chair, you know."

"But I haven't a gun," Teddy went on. He knew that he and Janet could make a tent, for they had often done it before.

"Couldn't you take a broom for a gun?" Janet asked. "I'll get it from the kitchen."

"Pooh! What good is a broom for a gun? I want one that shoots! Anyhow I haven't a uniform, and a soldier can't go to war without a uniform or a sword or a gun. I'm not going to play that!"

Janet did not know what to say for a few seconds. Truly a soldier would not be much of one without a gun or a uniform, even if he was in a tent. But the little girl had not given up yet.

The day was a rainy one. There was no school, for it was Saturday, and staying in the house was no great fun. Janet wanted her brother to stay and play with her and she knew she must do something to make him. For a while he had been content to play that he was Dr. Thompson, come to give medicine to Jan's sick doll. But Teddy had become tired of this after paying half a dozen visits and leaving pills made by rolling bread crumbs together.

Teddy laid aside his father's old hat and scratched his head. That is he tried to, but his head was so covered with tightly twisted curls that the little boy's fingers were fairly entangled in them.

"Say!" he exclaimed, "I wish my hair didn't curl so much! It's too long. I'm going to ask mother if I can't have it cut."

"I wish I could have mine cut," sighed Janet. "Mine's worse to comb than yours is, Ted."

3

"Yes, I know. And it always curls more on a rainy day."

Both children had the same curly hair. It was really beautiful, but they did not quite appreciate it, even though many of their friends, and some persons who saw them for the first time, called them "Curlytops." Indeed the tops of their heads were very curly.

"Oh, I know how we can do it!" suddenly cried Janet, just happening to think of something.

"Do what?" asked her brother.

"Play the soldier game. You can pretend you were caught by the enemy and your gun and uniform were taken away. Then you can be hurt and I'll be the Red Cross nurse and take care of you in the tent. I'll get some real sugar for pills, too! Nora'll give me some. She's in the kitchen now making a cake."

"Maybe she'd give you a piece of cake, too," suggested Teddy.

"Maybe," agreed Janet. "I'll go and ask her."

"Ask her for some chocolate," added Ted. "I guess, if I've got to be sick, I'd like chocolate pills 'stead of sugar."

"All right," said Janet, as she hurried downstairs from the playroom to the kitchen. In a little while she came back with a plate on which were two slices of chocolate cake, while on one edge of it were some crumbs of chocolate icing.

"I'll make pills of that after we eat the cake," Janet said. "You can pretend the cake made you sick if you want to, Ted."

"Pooh! who ever heard of a soldier getting sick on cake? Anyhow they don't have cake in the army — lessen they capture it from the enemy."

"Well, you can pretend you did that," said Janet. "Now I'll put my doll away," she went on, as she finished her piece of cake, "and we'll play the soldier game. I'll get some red cloth to make the cross."

Janet looked "sweet," as her mother said afterward, when she had wound a white cloth around her head, a red cross, rather ragged and crooked, being pinned on in front.

The tent was made by draping a sheet from the bed across two chairs, and under this shelter Teddy crawled. He stretched out on a blanket which Janet had spread on the floor to be the hospital cot.

"Now you must groan, Ted," she said, as she looked in a glass to see if her headpiece and cross were on straight.

"Groan? What for?"

"'Cause you've Been hurt in the war, or else you're sick from the cake."

"Pooh! a little bit of cake like that wouldn't make me sick. You've got to give me a lot more if you want me to be real sick."

"Oh, Teddy Martin! I'm not going to play if you make fun like that all the while. You've got to groan and pretend you've been shot. Never mind about the cake."

"All right. I'll be shot then. But you've got to give me a lot of chocolate pills to make me get better."

"I'm not going to give 'em to you all at once, Ted Martin!"

"Well, maybe in two doses then. How many are there?"

"Oh, there's a lot. I'm going to take some myself."

"You are not!" and Teddy sat up so quickly that he hit the top of the sheet-tent with his head and made it slide from the chair.

"There! Look what you did!" cried Janet. "Now you've gone and spoiled everything!"

"Oh, well, I'll fix it," said Ted, rather sorry for what he had done. "But you can't eat my chocolate pills."

"I can so!"

"You cannot! Who ever heard of a nurse taking the medicine from a sick soldier?"

5

"Well, anyhow—well, wouldn't you give me some chocolate candy if you had some, and I hadn't?" asked Janet.

"Course I would, Jan. I'm not stingy!"

"Well, these pills are just like chocolate candy, and if I give 'em all to you—"

"Oh, well, then I'll let you eat some," agreed Ted. "But you wanted me to play this game of bein' a sick soldier, and if I'm sick I've got to have the medicine."

"Yes, I'll give you the most," Janet agreed. "Now you lie down and groan and I'll hear you out on the battlefield and come and save your life."

So, after Janet had fixed the sheet over him again, Teddy lay back on the blanket and groaned his very best.

"Oh, it sounds as real as anything!" exclaimed the little girl in delight. "Do it some more, Ted!"

Thereupon her brother groaned more loudly until Janet stopped him by dropping two or three chocolate pills into his opened mouth.

"Oh! Gurr-r-r-r! Ugh! Say, you 'most choked me!" spluttered Ted, as he sat up and chewed the chocolate.

"Oh, I didn't mean to," said Janet as she ate a pill or two herself. "Now you lie down and go to sleep, 'cause I've got a lot more sick soldiers to go to see."

"Don't give 'em any of my chocolate pills," cautioned Ted. "I need 'em all to make me get better."

"I'll only make-believe give them some," promised Janet.

She and her brother played this game for a while, and Teddy liked it—as long as the chocolate pills were given him. But when Janet had only a few left and Teddy was about to say he was tired of lying down, someone came into the playroom and a voice asked:

"What you doin'?"

"Playing soldier," answered Janet. "You mustn't drop your 'g' letters, Trouble. Mother doesn't like it."

"I want some chocolate," announced the little boy, whose real name was William Martin, but who was more often called Trouble — because he got in so much of it, you know.

"There's only one pill left. Can I give it to him, Ted?" asked Janet.

"Yes, Janet. I've had enough. Anyhow, I know something else to play now. It's lots of fun!"

"What?" asked Janet eagerly. It was still raining hard and she wanted her brother to stay in the house with her.

"We'll play horse," went on Ted. "I'll be a bucking bronco like those Uncle Frank told us about on his ranch. We'll make a place with chairs where they keep the cow ponies and the broncos. I forget what Uncle Frank called it."

"I know," said Janet. "It's cor — corral."

"Corral!" exclaimed Ted. "That's it! We'll make a corral of some chairs and I'll be a bucking bronco. That's a horse that won't let anybody ride on its back," the little boy explained.

"I wants a wide!" said Baby William.

"Well, maybe I'll give you a ride after I get tired of bucking," said Teddy, thinking about it.

They made a ring of chairs on the playroom floor, and in this corral Teddy crept around on his hands and knees, pretending to be a wild Western pony. Janet tried to catch him and the children had much fun, Trouble screaming and laughing in delight.

At last Teddy allowed himself to be caught, for it was hard work crawling around as he did, and rearing up in the air every now and then.

"Give me a wide!" pleaded Trouble.

"Yes, I'll ride him on my back," offered Teddy, and his baby brother was put up there by Janet.

"Now don't go too fast with him, pony," she said.

"Yes, I wants to wide fast, like we does with Nicknack," declared Baby William. Nicknack was the Curlytops' pet goat.

"All right, I'll give you a fast ride," promised Teddy.

He began crawling about the room with Trouble on his back. The baby pretended to drive his "horse" by a string which Ted held in his mouth like reins.

"Go out in de hall—I wants a big wide," directed Trouble.

"All right," assented Teddy. Out into the hall he went and then forgetting, perhaps, that he had his baby brother on his back, Teddy began to buck— that is flop up and down.

"Oh—oh! 'top!" begged Trouble.

"I can't! I'm a Wild-West pony," explained Ted, bucking harder than ever.

He hunched himself forward on his hands and knees, and before he knew it he was at the head of the stairs. Then, just how no one could say, Trouble gave a yell, toppled off Teddy's back and the next instant went rolling down the flight, bump, bump, bumping at every step.

CHAPTER II

NICKNACK AND TROUBLE

"Oh, Teddy!" screamed Janet. "Oh, Trouble!"

Teddy did not answer at once. Indeed he had hard work not to tumble down the stairs himself after his little brother. Ted clung to the banister, though, and managed to save himself.

"Oh, he'll be hurt — terrible!" cried Janet, and she tried to get past her older brother to run downstairs after Trouble.

But Mrs. Martin, who was in the dining-room talking to Nora Jones, the maid, heard the noise and ran out into the hall.

"Oh, children!" she cried. "Teddy — Janet — what's all that noise?"

"It's Trouble, Mother!" announced Teddy. "I was playing bucking bronco and — "

"Trouble fell downstairs!" screamed Janet.

While everyone was thus calling out at once, Baby William came flopping head over heels, and partly sidewise, down the padded steps, landing right at his mother's feet, sitting up as straight as though in his high-chair.

"Oh, darling!" cried Mrs. Martin, catching the little fellow up in her arms, "are you hurt?"

Trouble was too much frightened to scream or cry. He had his mouth open but no sound came from it. He was just like the picture of a sobbing baby.

"Oh, Nora!" cried Mrs. Martin, as she hurried into the dining-room with her little boy in her arms. "Trouble fell downstairs! Get ready to telephone for his father and the doctor in case he's badly hurt," and then she and the maid began looking over Baby William to find out just what was the matter with him, while Ted and Janet, much frightened and very quiet, stood around waiting.

And while Mrs. Martin is looking over Trouble it will be a good chance for me to tell those of you who meet the Curlytops for the first time in this book something about them, and what has happened to them in the other volumes of this series.

The first book is named "The Curlytops at Cherry Farm," and in that I had the pleasure of telling you about Ted and Janet and Trouble Martin and their father and mother, when they went to Grandpa Martin's place, called Cherry Farm, which was near the village of Elmburg, not far from Clover Lake.

There the children found a goat, which they named Nicknack, and they kept him as a pet. When hitched to a wagon he gave them many nice rides. There were many cherry trees on Grandpa Martin's farm, and when some of the other crops failed the cherries were a great help, especially when the Lollypop Man turned them into "Chewing Cherry Candy."

After a good time on the farm the children had more fun when, as told in the second book, named "The Curlytops on Star Island," they went camping with grandpa. On Star Island in Clover Lake they saw a strange blue light which greatly puzzled them, and it was some time before they knew what caused it.

The summer and fall passed and Ted and Janet went home to Cresco, where they lived, to spend the winter. What happened then is told in the third volume, called "The Curlytops Snowed In." The big storm was so severe that no one could get out and even Nicknack was lost wandering about in the big drifts.

The Curlytops had a good time, even if they were snowed in. Now spring had come again, and the children were ready for something else. But I must tell you a little bit about the family, as well as about what happened.

You have already met Ted, Jan and Trouble. Ted's real name was Theodore, but his mother seldom called him that unless she was quite serious about something he had done that was wrong. So he was more often spoken to as Ted or Teddy, and his sister Janet was called Jan. Though oftener still they were called the "Curlytops," or, if one was speaking to one or the other he would say "Curlytop." That was because both Teddy and Janet had such very, very curly hair.

Ted's and Jan's birthdays came on the same day, but they had been born a year apart, Teddy being about seven years old and his sister a year younger. Trouble was aged about three years.

I have spoken of the curly hair of Teddy and Janet. Unless you had seen it you would never have believed hair could be so curly! It was no wonder that even strangers called the children "Curlytops."

Sometimes, when Mother Martin was combing the hair of the children, the comb would get tangled and she would have to pull a little to get it loose. That is one reason Ted never liked to have his hair combed. Janet's was a little longer than his, but just as curly.

Trouble's real name, as I have mentioned, was William. His father sometimes called him "A bunch of trouble," and his mother spoke of him as "Dear Trouble," while Jan and Ted called him just "Trouble."

Mr. Martin, whose name was Richard, shortened to Dick by his wife (whose name was Ruth) owned a store in Cresco, which is in one of our Eastern states.

Nora Jones, a cheerful, helpful maid-of-all-work had been in the Martin family a long while, and dearly loved the children, who were very fond of her. The Martins had many relatives besides the children's grandfather and grandmother, but I will only mention two now. They were Aunt Josephine Miller, called Aunt Jo, who lived at Clayton and who had a summer bungalow at Mt. Hope, near Ruby Lake. She was a sister of Mrs. Martin's. Uncle Frank Barton owned a large ranch near Rockville, Montana. He was Mr. Martin's uncle, but Ted and Janet also called him their uncle.

Now that you have met the chief members of the family, and know a little of what has happened to them in the past you may be interested to go back to see what the matter is with Trouble.

His mother turned him over and over in her arms, feeling of him here and there. Trouble had closed his mouth by this time, having changed his mind about crying. Instead he was very still and quiet.

"Trouble, does it hurt you anywhere?" his mother asked him anxiously.

"No," he said. "Not hurt any place. I wants to wide on Teddy's back some more."

"The little tyke!" exclaimed Mrs. Martin with a sigh of relief. "I don't believe he is hurt a bit."

"The stairs are real soft since we put the new carpet on them," remarked Nora.

"They are well padded," agreed Mrs. Martin. "I guess that's what kept him from getting hurt. It was like rolling down a feather bed. But he might have got his arm or leg twisted under him and have broken a bone. How did he happen to fall?"

"We were playing Red Cross nurse," began Janet, "and Ted was a soldier in a tent and—"

"But how could William fall downstairs if you were playing that sort of game?" asked her mother.

"Oh, we weren't playing it then," put in Ted. "We'd changed to another game. I was a wild Western bronco, like those on Uncle Frank's ranch, and I was giving Trouble a ride on my back. I gave a jump when I was near the stairs, and I guess he must have slipped off."

"There isn't any guessing about it—he did slip off," said Mrs. Martin with a smile, as she put Trouble in a chair, having made sure he was not hurt, and that there was no need of telephoning for his father or the doctor. "You must be more careful, Teddy. You might have hurt your little brother."

"Yes'm," Teddy answered. "I won't do it again."

"But we want to play something," put in Janet. "It's no fun being in the house all day."

"I know it isn't. But I think the rain is going to stop pretty soon. If you get your rain-coats and rubbers you may go out for a little while."

"Me go too?" begged Trouble.

"Yes, you may go too," agreed his mother. "You'll all sleep better if you get some fresh air; and it's warm, even if it has been raining."

"Maybe we can take Nicknack and have a ride!" exclaimed Teddy.

"If it stops raining," said his mother.

Ted, Jan and Trouble ran up and down in front of the house while the rain fell softly and the big drops dripped from the trees. Then the clouds broke away, the sun came out, the rain stopped and with shouts and laughter the children ran to the barn next to which, in a little stable of his own, Nicknack, the goat, was kept.

"Come on out, Nicknack!" cried Janet. "You're going to give us a ride!"

And Nicknack did, being hitched to the goat-cart in which there was room and to spare for Janet, Ted and Trouble. Up and down the street in front of their home the Martin children drove their pet goat.

"Whee, this is fun!" cried Ted, as he made Nicknack run downhill with the wagon.

"Oh, Teddy Martin, don't go so fast!" begged Janet.

"I like to go fast!" answered her brother. "I'm going to play Wild West. This is the stage coach and pretty soon the Indians will shoot at us!"

"Teddy Martin! if you're going to do that I'm not going to play!" stormed Janet. "You'll make Trouble fall out and get hurt. Come on, Trouble! Let us get out!" she cried. Nicknack was going quite fast down the hill.

"Wait till we get to the bottom," shouted Ted. "G'lang there, pony!" he cried to the goat.

"Let me out!" screamed Janet, "I want to get out."

At the foot of the hill Teddy stopped the goat and Janet, taking Trouble with her, got out and walked back to the house.

"What's the matter now?" asked Mrs. Martin from the porch where she had come out to get a little fresh air.

"Ted's playing Wild West in the goat-wagon," explained Janet.

"Oh, Ted! Don't be so rough!" begged his mother of her little son, who drove up just then.

"Oh, I'm only playing Indians and stage coach," he said. "You've got to go fast when the Indians are after you!" and away he rode.

"He's awful mean!" declared Janet.

"I don't know what's come over Ted of late," said Mrs. Martin to her husband, who came up the side street just then from his store.

"What's he been doing?" asked Mr. Martin.

"Oh, he's been pretending he was a bucking bronco, like those Uncle Frank has on his ranch, and he tossed Trouble downstairs. But the baby didn't get hurt, fortunately. Now Ted's playing Wild West stagecoach with Nicknack and Janet got frightened and wouldn't ride."

"Hum, I see," said Ted's father slowly. "Our boy is getting older, I guess. He needs rougher play. Well, I think I've just the very thing to suit him, and perhaps Janet and all of us."

"What is it?" asked Mrs. Martin, as her husband drew a letter from his pocket.

"This is an invitation from Uncle Frank for all of us to come out to his ranch in Montana for the summer," was the answer. "We have been talking of going, you know, and now is a good chance. I can leave the store for a while, and I think it would do us all good — the children especially — to go West. So if you'd like it, well pack up and go."

"Go where?" asked Ted, driving around near the veranda in time to hear his father's last words.

"Out to Uncle Frank's ranch," said Mr. Martin.

"How would you like that?" added his mother.

"Could we have ponies to ride?" asked Ted.

"Yes, I think so."

"Oh, what fun!" cried Janet. "I love a pony!"

"You'd be afraid of them!" exclaimed Ted.

"I would not! If they didn't jump up and down the way you did with Trouble on your back I wouldn't be afraid."

"Pooh! that's the way bucking broncos always do, don't they, Daddy? I'm going to have a bronco!"

"Well, well see when we get there," said Daddy Martin. "But since you all seem to like it, we'll go out West."

"Can we take Nicknack?" asked Teddy.

"You won't need him if you have a pony," his father suggested.

"No, that's so. Hurray! What fun we'll have!"

"Are there any Indians out there?" asked Janet.

"Well, a few, I guess," her father answered. "But they're docile Indians — not wild. They won't hurt you. Now let's go in and talk about it."

The Curlytops asked all sorts of questions of their father about Uncle Frank's ranch, but though he could tell them, in a general way, what it looked like, Mr. Martin did not really know much about the place, as he had never been there.

"But you'll find lots of horses, ponies and cattle there," he said.

"And can we take Nicknack with us, to ride around the ranch?" asked Jan, in her turn.

"Oh, you won't want to do that," her father said. "You'll have ponies to ride, I think."

"What'll we do with Nicknack then?" asked Ted.

"We'll have to leave him with some neighbor until we come back," answered his father. "I was thinking of asking Mr. Newton to take care of him. Bob Newton is a kind boy and he wouldn't harm your goat."

"Yes, Bob is a good boy," agreed Teddy. "I'd like him to have Nicknack."

"Then, if it is all right with Mr. Newton, well take the goat over a few days before we leave for the West," said Mr. Martin. "Bob will have a chance to get used to Nicknack, and Nicknack to him, before we go away."

"Nicknack not come wif us?" asked Trouble, not quite understanding what the talk was about.

"No, we'll leave Nicknack here," said his father, as he cuddled the little fellow up in his lap. Trouble said nothing more just then but, afterward, Ted remembered that Baby William seemed to be thinking pretty hard about something.

A few days later, when some of the trunks had been partly packed, ready for the trip West, Mr. Martin came home early from the store and said to Jan and Ted:

"I think you'd better get your goat ready now and take him over to Bob's house. I spoke to Mr. Newton about it, and he said there was plenty of room in his stable for a goat Bob is delighted to have him."

"But hell give him back to us when we come home, won't he?" asked Janet.

"Oh, yes, of course! You won't lose your goat," said her father with a laugh.

But when they went out to the stable to harness Nicknack to the wagon, Ted and Janet rubbed their eyes and looked again.

"Why, Nicknack is gone!" exclaimed Ted.

"He is," agreed his sister. "Maybe Bob came and got him."

"No, he wouldn't do that without telling us," went on Ted. "I wonder where that goat is?"

He looked around the stable yard and in the barn. No Nicknack was in sight.

When the Curlytops were searching they heard their mother calling to them from the house, where their father was waiting for them to come up with Nicknack. He was going over to Mr. Newton's with them.

"Ho, Ted! Janet! Where are you?" called Mrs. Martin.

"Out here, Mother!" Teddy answered.

"Is Trouble there with you?"

"Trouble? No, he isn't here!"

"He isn't!" exclaimed his mother. "Where in the world can he be? Nora says she saw him going out to the barn a little while ago. Please find him!"

"Huh!" exclaimed Ted. "Trouble is gone and so is Nicknack! I s'pose they've gone together!"

"Well have to look," said Janet.

CHAPTER III
OFF FOR THE WEST

The Curlytops hurried toward the house, leaving open the empty little stable in which Nicknack was usually kept. They found their father and their mother looking around in the yard, Mrs. Martin had a worried air.

"Couldn't you find him?" asked Daddy Martin.

"We didn't look—very much," answered Teddy. "Nicknack is gone, and—"

"Nicknack gone!" cried Mrs. Martin. "I wonder if that little tyke of ours has gotten into trouble with him."

"Nicknack wouldn't make any trouble," declared Jan. "He's such a nice goat—"

"Yes, I know!" said Mrs. Martin quickly. "But it looks very much as though Trouble and Nicknack had gone off together. Is the goat's harness in the stable?"

"We didn't look," answered Teddy.

"The wagon's gone," Janet said. "I looked under the shed for that and it wasn't there."

"Then I can just about guess what has happened," said Daddy Martin. "Trouble heard as talking about taking Nicknack over to Mr. Newton's house, where he would be kept while we are at Uncle Frank's ranch, and the little fellow has just about taken the goat over himself."

"Nonsense!" exclaimed Mrs. Martin. "Trouble couldn't hitch the goat to the wagon and drive off with him."

"Oh, yes he could, Mother!" said Teddy. "He's seen me and Janet hitch Nicknack up lots of times, and he's helped, too. At first he got the straps all crooked, but I showed him how to do it, and I guess he could 'most hitch the goat up himself now all alone."

"Then that's what he's done," said Mr. Martin. "Come on, Curlytops, we'll go over to Mr. Newton's and get Trouble."

"I hope you find him all right," said Mrs. Martin, with a sigh.

18

"Oh, we'll find him all right — don't worry," her husband answered.

Laughing among themselves at the trick Trouble had played, Janet, Teddy and Mr. Martin started for the home of Mr. Newton, which was three or four long streets away, toward the edge of the town.

On the way they looked here and there, in the yards of houses where the children often went to play.

"For," said Mr. Martin, "it might be possible that when Trouble found he could drive Nicknack, which he could do, as the goat is very gentle, he might have stopped on the way to play."

"Yes, he might," said Jan. "He's so cute!"

But there was no sign of the little boy, nor the goat, either.

Finally Mr. Newton's house was reached. Into the yard rushed Janet and Teddy, followed by their father. Bob Newton was making a kite on the side porch.

"Hello, Curlytop!" he called to Ted. "Want to help me fly this? It's going to be a dandy!"

"Yes, I'll help you," agreed Ted. "But is he here?"

"Who here?" asked Bob, in some surprise.

"Nicknack, our goat," answered Teddy.

"What! Is he lost?" exclaimed Bob in some dismay, for he was counting on having much fun with the goat when the Curlytops went West.

"Nicknack —" began Ted.

"Have you seen Trouble?" broke in Janet.

"Is he lost, too?" Bob inquired. "Say, I guess —"

"Our goat and little boy seem to have gone off together," explained Mr. Martin to Mrs. Newton who came out on the porch just then. "We'd been talking before Trouble about bringing Nicknack over here, and now that both are missing we thought maybe Baby William had brought the goat over himself."

"Why, no, he isn't here," said Mrs. Newton slowly. "You didn't see anything of Trouble and the goat, did you?" she asked her son.

"No. I've been here making the kite all morning, and I'd have seen Nicknack all right, and Trouble, too, if they had come here."

"Well, that's funny!" exclaimed Mr. Martin. "I wonder where he can have gone?"

"Maybe Nicknack ran away with him," suggested Bob.

"Oh, don't say such things!" exclaimed his mother.

"I don't think that can have happened," returned Mr. Martin, "Nicknack is a very gentle goat, and Trouble is used to playing with him all alone. He never yet has been hurt. Of course we are not sure that the two went away together. Trouble disappeared from the house, and he was last seen going toward the stable.

"When Ted and Jan went out to get Nicknack he was gone, too, and so was the wagon and harness. So we just thought Trouble might have driven his pet over here."

"Yes, I think it likely that the two went away together," said Mrs. Newton; "but they're not here. Bob, put away that kite of yours and help Mr. Martin and the Curlytops look for Trouble. He may have gone to Mrs. Simpson's," she went on. "He's often there you know."

"Yes, but we looked in their yard coming over," put in Ted. "Trouble wasn't there."

"That's strange," murmured Bob's mother. "Well, he can't be far, that's sure, and he can't get lost. Everybody in town knows him and the goat, and he's sure to be seen sooner or later."

"I guess so," agreed Mr. Martin. "His mother was a little worried, though."

"Yes, I should think she would be. It's horrible to have anything happen to your children—or fear it may. I'll take off my apron and help you look."

"Oh, don't bother," said Mr. Martin. "We'll find him all right." But Mrs. Newton insisted on joining the search.

There was a barn on the Newton place—a barn in which Bob was counting on keeping Nicknack—and this place was first searched lest, perchance, Trouble might have slipped in there with the goat without anyone having seen him, having come up through a back alley.

But there was no goat inside; and Bob, the Curlytops, Mr. Martin and Mrs. Newton came out again, and looked up and down the street.

"I'll tell you what we'd better do," said Bob's mother. "Ted, you come with Bob and me. You know Trouble's ways, and where he would be most likely to go. Let Janet go with her father, and we'll go up and down the street, inquiring in all the houses we come to. Your little brother is sure to be near one of them."

"That's a good idea," said Mr. Martin. "Jan, you come with me. I expect your mother will be along any minute now. She won't wait at home long for us if we don't come back with Trouble."

So the two parties started on the search, one up and the other down the street. Bob, Teddy and Mrs. Newton inquired at a number of houses, but no one in them had seen Trouble and Nicknack that day. Nor did Janet and her father get any trace of the missing ones.

"I wonder where he is," murmured Teddy, and he was beginning to feel afraid that something had happened to Trouble.

"Let's go down the back street," suggested Bob. "You know there's quite a lot of wagons and automobiles go along this main street where we've been looking. Maybe if Trouble hitched up Nicknack and went for a ride he'd turn down the back street 'cause it's quieter."

"Yes, he may have done that," agreed Mrs. Newton.

So down the back street the three went. There were several vacant lots on this street and as the grass in them was high—tall enough to hide a small boy and a goat and wagon—Bob said they had better look in these places.

This they did. There was nothing in the first two vacant lots, but in the third—after they had stopped at one or two houses and had not found the missing ones—Teddy suddenly cried out:

"Hark!"

"What'd you hear?" asked Bob.

"I thought I heard a goat bleating," was the answer.

"Listen!" whispered Mrs. Newton.

They kept quiet, and then through the air came the sound:

"Baa-a-a-a-a!"

"That's Nicknack!" cried Teddy, rushing forward.

"I hope your little brother is there, too," said Mrs. Newton.

And Trouble was. When they got to the lower end of the vacant lot there, in a tangle of weeds, was the goat-wagon, and Nicknack was in a tangle of harness fast to it.

"Look at Trouble!" cried Teddy.

There lay the little fellow, sound asleep in the goat-wagon, his head pillowed on his arm, while Nicknack was bleating now and then between the bites of grass and weeds he was eating.

"Oh, Trouble!" cried Mrs. Newton as she took him up in her arms.

"Yes—dis me—I's Trouble," was the sleepy response. "Oh, 'lo, Teddy," he went on as he saw his brother. "'Lo, Bob. You come to find me?"

"I should say we did!" cried Bob. "What are you doing here?"

"Havin' wide," was the answer. "Everybody go 'way—out West—I not have a goat den. I no want Nicknack to go 'way."

"Oh, I see what he means!" exclaimed Teddy, after thinking over what his little brother said. "He heard us talking about bringing Nicknack over to your house, Bob, to keep him for us. Trouble likes the goat and I guess he didn't want to leave him behind. Maybe he thought he could drive him away out to Montana, to Uncle Frank's ranch."

"Maybe," agreed Bob. "That'd be a long drive, though."

"I should say so!" agreed Mrs. Newton. "But I guess you're right, Teddy. Your little brother started off to hide the goat and wagon so you couldn't leave it behind. He's a funny baby, all right!"

"And look how he harnessed him!" exclaimed Bob.

Nicknack really wasn't harnessed. The leather straps and the buckles were all tangled up on him, but Trouble had managed to make enough of them stick on the goat's back, and had somehow got part of the harness fast to the wagon, so Nicknack could pull it along.

"I had a nice wide," said Trouble, as Bob and Teddy straightened out the goat's harness. "Den I got sleepy an' Nicknack he got hungry, so we comed in here."

"And we've been looking everywhere for you!" exclaimed Mrs. Newton. "Well, I'm glad we've found you. Come along, now. Ted, you and Bob hurry along and tell the others. Your mother'll be worried."

And indeed Mrs. Martin was worried, especially when she met Mr. Martin and Janet, who had not found Trouble.

But Teddy and Bob soon met with the other searchers and told them that Baby "William had been found.

"Oh, what will you do next?" cried Mrs. Martin, as she clasped the little fellow in her arms. "Such a fright as you've given us!"

"No want Nicknack to go 'way!" said Trouble.

"I guess that's what he did it for—he thought he could hide the goat so we wouldn't leave him behind," said Daddy Martin. "But we'll have to, just the same. Trouble won't miss him when we get out on the ranch."

So the goat and wagon were left at Bob's house, and though Trouble cried when he realized what was happening, he soon got over it.

The next few days were filled with busy preparations toward going West. Daddy Martin bought the tickets, the packing was completed, last visits to their playmates were paid by Janet and Teddy, whose boy and girl friends all said that they wished they too were going out West to a big ranch.

"We're going to see cowboys and Indians!" Ted told everyone.

Then came the last day in Cresco — that is the last day for some time for the Curlytops. The house was closed, Nora going to stay with friends. Skyrocket, the dog, and Turnover, the cat, were sent to kind neighbors, who promised to look after them. Bob had already started to take care of Nicknack.

"All aboard!" called the conductor of the train the Curlytops and the others took. "All aboard!"

"All aboard for the West!" echoed Daddy Martin, and they were off.

CHAPTER IV
THE COLLISION

"Won't we have fun, Jan, when we get to the ranch?"

"I guess so, Teddy. But I don't like it about those Indians."

"Oh, didn't you hear Daddy say they were tame ones — like the kind in the circus and Wild West show? They won't hurt you, Jan."

"Well, I don't like 'em. They've got such funny painted faces."

"Not the tame ones, Jan. Anyhow I'll stay with you."

The Curlytops were talking as they sat together in the railroad car which was being pulled rapidly by the engine out toward the big West, where Uncle Frank's ranch was. In the seat behind them was Mother Martin, holding Trouble, who was asleep, while Daddy Martin was also slumbering.

It was quite a long ride from Cresco to Rockville, which was in Montana. It would take the Curlytops about four days to make the trip, perhaps longer if the trains were late. But they did not mind, for they had comfortable coaches in which to travel. When they were hungry there was the dining-car where they could get something to eat, and when they were sleepy there was the sleeping-car, in which the colored porter made such funny little beds out of the seats.

Jan and Ted thought it quite wonderful. For, though they had traveled in a sleeping-car before, and had seen the porter pull out the seats, let down the shelf overhead and take out the blankets and pillows to make the bed, still they never tired of watching.

There were many other things to interest the Curlytops and Trouble on this journey to Uncle Frank's ranch. Of course there was always something to see when they looked out of the windows of the cars. At times the train would pass through cities, stopping at the stations to let passengers get off and on. But it was not the cities that interested the children most. They liked best to see the fields and woods through which they passed.

In some of the fields were horses, cows or sheep, and while the children did not see any such animals in the woods, except perhaps where the wood was a clump of trees near a farm, they always hoped they might.

Very often, when the train would rattle along through big fields, and then suddenly plunge into a forest, Jan would call:

"Maybe we'll see one now, Ted!"

"Oh, maybe so!" he would exclaim.

Then the two Curlytops would flatten their noses against the window and peer out.

"What are you looking for?" asked Mother Martin, the first time she saw the children do this.

"Indians," answered Teddy, never turning around, for the train was still in the wood and he did not want to miss any chance.

"Indians!" exclaimed his mother, "Why, what in the world put into your head the idea that we should see Indians?"

"Well, Uncle Frank said there were Indians out West, even if they weren't wild ones," answered Teddy, "and me and Jan wants to see some."

"Oh, you won't find any Indians around here," said Daddy Martin with a laugh, as he laid aside the paper he was reading. "It is true there are some out West, but we are not there yet, and, if we were, you would hardly find the Indians so near a railroad."

"Can't we ever see any?" Jan wanted to know. "I don't just like Indians, 'cause they've always got a gun or a knife—I mean in pictures," she hastened to add. "Course I never saw a real Indian, 'ceptin' maybe in a circus."

"You'll see some real ones after a while," her mother told her, and then the children stopped pressing their noses flat against the car windows, for the train had come out of the wood and was nearing a large city. There, Jan and Ted felt sure, no Indians would be seen.

"But we'll keep watch," said Jan to her brother, "and maybe I'll see an Indian first."

"And maybe I will! We'll both watch!" he agreed.

Something else that gave the children enjoyment was the passage through the train, every now and then, of the boy who sold candy, books and magazines. He would pass along between the seats, dropping into them, or into the laps of the passengers, packages of candy, or perhaps a paper or book. This was to give the traveler time to look at it, and make up his or her mind whether or not to buy it.

A little later the boy would come along to collect the things he had left, and get the money for those the people kept for themselves. Ted and Jan were very desirous, each time, that the boy should sell something, and once, when he had gone through the car and had taken in no money, he looked so disappointed that Jan whispered to her father:

"Won't you please buy something from him?"

"Buy what?" asked Mr. Martin.

"A book or some candy from the newsboy," repeated the little girl. "He looks awful sorry."

"Hum! Well, it is too bad if he didn't sell anything," said Mr. Martin. "I guess I can buy something. What would you like, something to read or something to eat?"

"Some pictures to look at," suggested Teddy. "Then we can show 'em to Trouble. Mother just gave us some cookies."

"Then I guess you've had enough to eat," laughed Mr. Martin. "Here, boy!" he called. "Have you any picture books for these Curlytops of mine?"

"Yes, I have some nice ones," answered the boy, and with a smile on his face he went into the baggage car, where he kept his papers, candy and other things, and soon came back with a gaily colored book, at the sight of which Ted and Jan uttered sighs of delight.

"Dat awful p'etty!" murmured Trouble, and indeed the book did have nice pictures in it.

Mr. Martin paid for it, and then Ted and Jan enjoyed very much looking at it, with Trouble in the seat between them. He insisted on seeing each picture twice, the page being no sooner turned over than he wanted it turned back again.

But at last even he was satisfied, and then Ted and Jan went back to their first game of looking out of the window for Indians or other sights that might interest them.

Trouble slipped out of his seat between his brother and sister and went to a vacant window himself. For a time he had good fun playing with the window catch, and Mrs. Martin let him do this, having made sure, at first, that he could not open the sash. Then they all forgot Trouble for a while and he played by himself, all alone in one of the seats.

A little later, when Teddy and Janet were tired of looking for the Indians which they never saw, they were talking about the good times they had had with Nicknack, and wondering if Uncle Frank would have a goat, or anything like it, when Trouble came toddling up to their seat.

"What you got?" asked Teddy of his little brother, noticing that Baby William was chewing something. "What you got, Trouble?"

"Tandy," he said, meaning candy, of course.

"Oh, where'd you get it?" chimed in Jan.

"Nice boy gived it to me," Trouble answered. "Here," and he held the package out to his brother and sister.

"Oh, wasn't that good of him!" exclaimed Jan. "It's nice chocolate candy, too. I'll have another piece, Trouble."

They all had some and they were eating the sweet stuff and having a good time, when they saw their father looking at them. There was a funny smile on his face, and near him stood the newsboy, also smiling.

"Trouble, did you open a box of candy the boy left in your seat?" asked Mr. Martin.

"Yes, he's got some candy," answered Jan. "He said the boy gave it to him."

"I didn't mean for him to open it," the boy said. "I left it in his seat and I thought he'd ask his father if he could have it. But when I came to get it, why, it was gone."

"Oh, what a funny little Trouble!" laughed Mother Martin. "He thought the boy meant to give the candy to him, I guess. Well, Daddy, I think you'll have to pay for it."

And so Mr. Martin did. The candy was not a gift after all, but Trouble did not know that. However, it all came out right in the end.

They had been traveling two days, and now, toward evening of the second day, the Curlytops were talking together about what they would do when they got to Uncle Frank's ranch.

"I hope they have lots to eat there," sighed Ted, when he and Jan had gotten off the subject of Indians. "I'm hungry right now."

"So'm I," added his sister. "But they'll call us to supper pretty soon."

The children always eagerly waited for the colored waiter to come through the coaches rumbling out in his bass voice:

"First call fo' supper in de dinin'-car!"

Or he might say "dinner" or "breakfast," or make it the "last call," just as it happened. Now it was time for the first supper call, and in a little while the waiter came in.

"Eh? What's that? Time for supper again?" cried Daddy Martin, awakening from a nap.

Trouble stretched and yawned in his mother's arms.

"I's hungry!" he said.

"So'm I!" cried Ted and Jan together.

"Shall we have good things to eat on Uncle Frank's ranch?" asked Teddy, as they made ready to walk ahead to the dining-car.

"Of course!" his mother laughed. "Why are you worrying about that?"

"Oh, I just wanted to know," Teddy answered. "We had so many good things at Cherry Farm and when we were camping with grandpa that I want some out on the ranch."

"Well, I think we can trust to Uncle Frank," said Mr. Martin. "But if you get too hungry, Teddy, you can go out and lasso a beefsteak or catch a bear or deer and have him for breakfast."

"Is there bears out there, too?" asked Janet in a good deal of excitement. "Bears and Indians?"

"Well, there may be a few bears here and there," her father said with a smile, "but they won't hurt you if you don't hurt them. Now we'll go and see what they have for supper here."

To the dining-car they went, and as they passed through one of the coaches on their way Teddy and Janet heard a woman say to her little girl:

"Look at those Curlytops, Ethel. Don't you wish you could have some of their curl put into your hair?"

It was evening and the sun was setting. As the train sped along the Curlytops could look through the windows off across the fields and woods through which they passed.

"Isn't it just wonderful," said Mother Martin, "to think of sitting down to a nice meal which is being cooked for us while the train goes so fast? Imagine, children, how, years ago, the cowboys and hunters had to go on horses all the distance out West, and carry their food on their pony's back or in a wagon called a prairie schooner. How much easier and quicker and more comfortable it is to travel this way."

"I'd like to ride on a pony," said Teddy. "I wouldn't care how slow he went."

"I imagine you wouldn't like it when night came," said his mother, as she moved a plate so the waiter could set glasses of milk in front of the children. "You wouldn't like to sleep on the ground with only a blanket for a bed, would you?"

"'Deed I would!" declared Teddy. "I wish I had—"

Just then the train went around a curve, and, as it was traveling very fast, the milk which Teddy was raising to his mouth slopped and spilled down in his lap.

"Oh, Teddy!" cried his mother.

"I—I couldn't help it!" he exclaimed, as he wiped up as much of the milk as he could on a napkin with which the waiter hastened to him.

"No, we know it was the train," said Daddy Martin. "It wouldn't have happened if you had been traveling on pony-back, and had stopped to camp out for the night before you got your supper; would it, Ted?" he asked with a smile.

"No," said the little boy. "I wish we could camp out and hunt Indians!"

"Oh my goodness!" exclaimed his mother. "Don't get such foolish notions in your head. Anyway there aren't any Indians to hunt on Uncle Frank's ranch, are there, Dick?" she asked her husband.

"Well, no, I guess not," he answered slowly. "There are some Indians on their own ranch, or government reservation, not far from where Uncle Frank has his horses and cattle, but I guess the Redmen never bother anyone."

"Can we go to see 'em?" asked Teddy.

"I guess so," said Mr. Martin.

"Me go, too! Me like engines," murmured Trouble, who had also spilled a little milk on himself.

"He thinks we're talking about engines—the kind that pull this train!" laughed Ted. "I don't believe he ever saw a real Indian."

"No, Indians do not walk the streets of Cresco," said Mrs. Martin. "But finish your suppers, children. Others are waiting to use the table and we must not keep them too long."

There were many travelers going West—not all as far as the Curlytops though—and as there was not room in the dining-car for all of them to sit down at once they had to take turns. That is why the waiter made one, two, and sometimes three calls for each meal, as he went through the different coaches.

Supper over, the Martins went back to their place in the coach in which they had ridden all day. They would soon go into the beds, or berths, as they are called, to sleep all night. In the morning they would be several hundred miles nearer Uncle Frank's ranch.

The electric lights were turned on, and then, for a while, Jan, Ted and the others sat and talked.

They talked about the fun they had had when at Cherry Farm, of the good times camping with grandpa and how they were snowed in, when they wondered what had become of the strange lame boy who had called at Mr. Martin's store one day.

"I wish Hal Chester could come out West with us" said Teddy, as the porter came to tell them he would soon make up their beds. "He'd like to hunt Indians with me."

Hal was a boy who had been cured of lameness at a Home for Crippled Children, not far from Cherry Farm.

"I suppose you'll dream of Indians," said Teddy's mother to him. "You've talked about them all day. But get ready for bed, now. Traveling is tiresome for little folks."

Indeed after the first day Ted and Janet found it so. They wished, more than once, that they could get out and run about, but they could not except when the train stopped longer than usual in some big city. Then their father would take them to the platform for a little run up and down.

True they could walk up and down the aisle of the car, but this was not much fun, as the coach swayed so they were tossed against the sides of the seats and bruised.

"I'll be glad when we get to Uncle Frank's ranch," said Janet as she crawled into the berth above her mother, who slept with Trouble.

"So'll I," agreed Teddy, who climbed up the funny little ladder to go to bed in the berth above his father. "I want a pony ride!"

On through the night rumbled and roared the train, the whistle sounding mournfully in the darkness as the engineer blew it at the crossings.

Ted and Janet were sleeping soundly, Janet dreaming she had a new doll, dressed like an Indian papoose, or baby, while Ted dreamed he was on a wild pony that wanted to roll over and over instead of galloping straight on.

Suddenly there was a loud crash that sounded through the whole train. The engine whistled shrilly and then came a jar that shook up everyone. Teddy found himself rolling out of his berth and he grabbed the curtains just in time to save himself.

"Oh, Daddy!" he cried, "what's the matter?"

"What is it?" called Jan from her berth, while women in the coach were screaming and men ere calling to one another.

"What is it, Dick?" cried Mrs. Martin.

"I think we've had a collision," answered her husband.

"Did our train bunk into another?" asked Ted.

"I'm afraid so," replied his father.

CHAPTER V
AT RING ROSY RANCH

There was so much noise in the sleeping car where the Curlytops and others had been peacefully traveling through the night, that, at first, it was hard to tell what had happened.

All that anyone knew was that there had been a severe jolt—a "bunk" Teddy called it—and that the train had come to a sudden stop. So quickly had it stopped, in fact, that a fat man, who was asleep in a berth just behind Mr. Martin, had tumbled out and now sat in the aisle of the car, gazing about him, a queer look on his sleepy face, for he was not yet fully awake.

"I say!" cried the fat man. "Who pushed me out of bed?"

Even though they were much frightened, Mrs. Martin and some of the other men and women could not help laughing at this. And the laughter did more to quiet them than anything else.

"Well, I guess no one here is much hurt—if at all," said Daddy Martin, as he put on a pair of soft slippers he had ready in the little hammock that held his clothes inside the berth. "I'll go and see if I can find out what the matter is."

"An', Daddy, bring me suffin t'eat!" exclaimed Trouble, poking his head out between the curtains of the berth where he had been sleeping with his mother when the collision happened.

"There's one boy that's got sense," said a tall thin man, who was helping the fat man to get to his feet "He isn't hurt, anyhow."

"Thank goodness, no," said Mrs. Martin, who, as had some of the other women, had on a dressing gown. Mrs. Martin was looking at Trouble, whom she had taken up in her arms. "He hasn't a scratch on him," she said, "though I heard him slam right against the side of the car. He was next to the window."

"It's a mercy we weren't all of us tossed out of the windows when the train stopped so suddenly, the way it did," said a little old woman.

"It's a mercy, too," smiled another woman who had previously made friends with Jan and Teddy, "that the Curlytops did not come hurtling down out of those upper berths."

Mr. Martin, after making sure his family was all right, partly dressed and went out with some of the other men. The train had come to a standstill, and Jan and Ted, looking out of the windows of their berths, could see men moving about in the darkness outside with flaring torches.

"Maybe it's robbers," said Teddy in a whisper.

"Robbers don't stop trains," objected Janet

"Yes they do!" declared her brother positively, "Train robbers do. Don't they, Mother?"

"Oh, don't talk about such things now, Teddy boy. Be thankful you are all right and hope that no one is hurt in the collision."

"That's what I say!" exclaimed the fat man. "So it's a collision, is it? I dreamed we were in a storm and that I was blown out of bed."

"Well, you fell out, which is much the same thing," said the thin man. "Our car doesn't seem to be hurt, anyhow."

Ted and Janet came out into the aisle in their pajamas. They looked all about them but, aside from seeing a number of men and women who were greatly excited, nothing else appeared to be the matter. Then in came their father with some of the other men.

"It isn't a bad collision," said Daddy Martin. "Our engine hit a freight car that was on a side track, but too close to our rails to be passed safely. It jarred up our engine and the front cars quite a bit, and our engine is off the track, but no one is hurt."

"That's good!" exclaimed Mrs. Martin. "I mean that no one is hurt."

"How are they going to get the engine back on the track?" Teddy wanted to know. "Can't I go out and watch 'em?"

"I want to go, too!" exclaimed Janet.

"Indeed you can't—in the dark!" exclaimed her father. "Besides, the railroad men don't want you in the way. They asked us all to go to our coaches and wait. They'll soon have the engine back on the rails they said."

Everyone was awake now, and several children in the car, like Trouble, were hungry. The porter who had been hurrying to and fro said he could get the children some hot milk from the dining-car, and this he did.

Some of the grown folks wanted coffee and sandwiches, and these having been brought in, there was quite a merry picnic in the coach, even if the train had been in a collision.

Then there was much puffing and whistling of the engine. The Curlytops, looking out of the window again, saw more men hurrying here and there with flaring torches which flickered and smoked. These were the trainmen helping to get the engine back on the rails, which they did by using iron wedges or "jumpers," much as a trolley car in your city streets is put back on the rails once it slips off.

At last there was another "bunk" to the train, as Teddy called it. At this several women screamed.

"It's all right," said Daddy Martin. "They've got the engine back on the rails and it has just backed up to couple on, or fasten itself, to the cars again. Now we'll go forward again."

And they did—in a little while. It did not take the Curlytops or Trouble long to fall asleep once more, but some of the older people were kept awake until morning, they said afterward. They were afraid of another collision.

But none came, and though the train was a little late the accident really did not amount to much, though it might have been a bad one had the freight car been a little farther over on the track so the engine had run squarely into it.

All the next day and night the Curlytops traveled in the train, and though Jan and Ted liked to look out of the windows, they grew tired of this after a while and began to ask:

"When shall we be at Uncle Frank's ranch?"

"Pretty soon now," said their father.

I will not tell you all that happened on the journey to the West. Truth to say there was not much except the collision. The Curly-tops ate their meals, drank cupful after cupful of water, and Trouble did the same, for children seem to get very thirsty when they travel—much more so than at home.

Then, finally, one afternoon, after a long stop when a new engine was attached to the train, Daddy Martin said:

"Well be at Rockville in an hour now. So we'd better begin to get together our things."

"Shall we be at Uncle Frank's ranch in an hour?" asked Teddy.

"No, but well be at Rockville. From there we go out over the prairies in a wagon."

"A wagon with ponies?" asked Janet.

"Yes, real Western ponies," said her father. "Then well be at the ranch."

And it happened just that way. On puffed the train. Then the porter came to help the Martin family off at Rockville.

"Rockville! Rockville! All out for Rockville!" joked Daddy Martin.

"Hurray!" cried Teddy. "Here we are!"

"And I see Uncle Frank!" exclaimed Janet, looking from the window toward the station as the train slowed up to stop.

Out piled the Curlytops, and into the arms of Uncle Frank they rushed. He caught them up and kissed them one after the other—Teddy, Janet and Trouble.

"Well, well!" he cried, "I'm glad to see you! Haven't changed a bit since you were snowed in! Now pile into the wagon and well get right out to Circle O Ranch."

"Where's that?" asked Teddy.

"Why, that's the name of my ranch," said Uncle Frank. "See, there's the sign of it," and he pointed to the flank of one of the small horses, or ponies, hitched to his wagon. Ted and Janet saw a large circle in which was a smaller letter O.

"We call it Circle O," explained the ranchman. "Each place in the West that raises cattle or horses has a certain sign with which the animals are branded, or marked, so their owners can tell them from others in case they get mixed up. My mark is a circle around an O."

"It looks like a ring-around-the-rosy," said Janet.

"Say! So it does!" laughed Uncle Frank. "I never thought of that. Ring Rosy Ranch! That isn't a half bad name! Guess I'll call mine that after this. Come on to Ring Rosy Ranch!" he invited as he laughed at the Curlytops.

And the name Janet gave Uncle Frank's place in fun stuck to it, so that even the cowboys began calling their ranch "Ring Rosy," instead of "Circle O."

CHAPTER VI
COWBOY FUN

Into the big wagon piled the Curlytops, Mrs. Martin and Trouble, while Daddy Martin and Uncle Frank went to see about the baggage.

Jan and Ted looked curiously about them. It was the first time they had had a chance to look quietly since they had started on the journey, for they had been traveling in the train nearly a week, it seemed.

What they saw was a small railroad station, set in the midst of big rolling fields. There was a water tank near the station, and not far from the tank was a small building in which a pump could be heard chug-chugging away.

"But where is the ranch?" asked Janet of her brother. "I don't see any cows and horses."

"Dere's horses," stated Trouble, pointing to the two sturdy ponies hitched to the wagon.

"Yes, I know" admitted Janet. "But Uncle Frank said he had more'n a hundred horses and—"

"And a thousand steers—that's cattle," interrupted Ted. "I don't see any, either. Maybe we got off at the wrong station, Mother."

"No, you're all right," laughed Mrs. Martin. "Didn't Uncle Frank meet us and didn't Daddy tell us we'd have to drive to the ranch?"

"What's the matter now, Curlytops?" asked their father's uncle, as the two men came back from having seen about the baggage, which had arrived safely. "What are you two youngsters worrying about, Teddy and Janet?"

"They're afraid we're at the wrong place because they can't see the ranch," answered their mother.

"Oh, that's over among the hills," said Uncle Frank, waving his hand toward some low hills that were at the foot of some high mountains. "It wouldn't do," he went on, "to have a ranch too near a railroad station. The trains might scare the horses and cattle. You will soon be there, Curlytops. We'll begin to travel in a minute."

Ted and Janet settled themselves in the seat, where they were side by side, and looked about them. Suddenly Janet clasped her brother by the arm and exclaimed:

"Look, Ted! Look!"

"Where?" he asked.

"Right over there—by the station. It's an Indian!"

"A real one?" asked Teddy, who, at first, did not see where his sister was pointing.

"He looks like a real one," Janet answered. "He's alive, 'cause he's moving!"

She snuggled closer to her brother. Then Teddy saw where Janet pointed. A big man, whose face was the color of a copper cent, was walking along the station platform. He was wrapped in a dirty blanket, but enough of him could be seen to show that he was a Redman.

"Is that a real Indian, Uncle Frank?" asked Teddy in great excitement.

"What? Him? Oh, yes, he's a real Indian all right. There's a lot of 'em come down to the station to sell baskets and beadwork to the people who go through on the trains."

"Is he a tame Indian?" the little boy next wanted to know.

"Oh, he's 'tame' all right. Hi there, Running Horse!" called Uncle Frank to the copper-faced man in the blanket, "sell many baskets to-day?"

"Um few. No good business," answered the Indian in a sort of grunt.

"Oh, do you know him?" asked Ted in surprise.

"Oh, yes. Running Horse often comes to the ranch when he's hungry. There's a reservation of the Indians not far from our place. They won't hurt you, Jan; don't be afraid," said Uncle Frank, as he saw that the little girl kept close to Teddy.

"Was he wild once?" she asked timidly.

"Why, yes; I guess you might have called him a wild Indian once," her uncle admitted. "He's pretty old and I shouldn't wonder but what he had been on the warpath against the white settlers."

"Oh!" exclaimed Janet. "Maybe he'll get wild again!"

"Oh, no he won't!" laughed Uncle Frank. "He's only too glad now to live on the reservation and sell the baskets the squaws make. The Indian men don't like to work."

Running Horse, which was the queer name the Indian had chosen for himself, or which had been given him, walked along, wrapped in his blanket, though the day was a warm one. Perhaps he thought the blanket kept the heat out in summer and the cold in winter.

"Get along now, ponies!" cried Uncle Frank, and the little horses began to trot along the road that wound over the prairies like a dusty ribbon amid the green grass.

On the way to Ring Rosy Ranch Uncle Frank had many questions to ask, some of the children and some of Mr. and Mrs. Martin. Together they laughed about the things that had happened when they were all snowed in.

"Tell Uncle Frank of Trouble's trying to hide Nicknack away so we wouldn't leave him behind," suggested Mrs. Martin.

"Ha! Ha! That was pretty good!" exclaimed the ranchman when Ted and Janet, by turns, had told of Trouble's being found asleep in the goat-wagon. "Well, it's too bad you couldn't bring Nicknack with you. He'd like it out on the ranch, I'm sure, but it would be too long a journey for him. You'll have rides enough — never fear!"

"Pony rides?" asked Teddy.

"Pony rides in plenty!" laughed Uncle Frank. "We'll soon be there now, and you can see the ranch from the top of the next hill."

The prairies were what are called "rolling" lard. That is there were many little hills and hollows, and the country seemed to be like the rolling waves of the ocean, if they had suddenly been made still.

41

Sometimes the wagon, drawn by the two little horses, would be down in a hollow, and again it would be on top of a mound-like hill from which a good view could be had.

Reaching the top of one hill, larger than the others, Uncle Frank pointed off in the distance and said:

"There's Circle O Ranch, Curlytops, or, as Jan has named it, Ring Rosy Ranch. We'll be there in a little while."

The children looked. They saw, off on the prairie, a number of low, red buildings standing close together. Beyond the buildings were big fields, in which were many small dots.

"What are the dots?" asked Janet.

"Those are my horses and cattle—steers we call the last," explained Uncle Frank.

"They are eating grass to get fat You'll soon be closer to them."

"Are the Indians near here?" Teddy inquired.

"No, not very near. It's a day's ride to their reservation. But don't worry about them. They won't bother you if you don't bother them," said Uncle Frank.

Teddy was not fully satisfied with this answer, for he hoped very much that the Indians would "bother him"—at least, he thought that was what he wanted.

When the Curlytops drew closer to the ranch they could see that one of the buildings was a house, almost like their own in the East, only not so tall. It was all one story, as were the other buildings, some of which were stables for the horses and some sleeping places, or "bunk houses," for the cowboys, while from one building, as they approached closer, there came the good smell of something cooking.

"That's the cook's place," said Uncle Frank, pointing with his whip. "All the cowboys love him, even if he is a Chinaman."

"Have you a Chinese cook?" asked Mrs. Martin.

"Yes, and he's a good one," answered Uncle Frank. "Wait until you taste how he fries chicken."

"I hope we taste some soon," said Daddy Martin. "This ride across the prairies has made me hungry."

"I hungry, too!" exclaimed Trouble. "I wants bread an' milk!"

"And you shall have all you want!" laughed the ranchman. "We've plenty of milk."

"Oh, this is a dandy place!" exclaimed Teddy, as the wagon drove up to the ranch house. "Well have lots of fun here, Janet!"

"Maybe we will, if — if the Indians don't get us," she said.

"Pooh! I'm not afraid of them," boasted Teddy, and then something happened.

All at once there came a lot of wild yells, and sounds as if a Fourth-of-July celebration of the old-fashioned sort were going on. There was a popping and a banging, and then around the corner of the house rode a lot of roughly-dressed men on ponies which kicked up a cloud of dust.

"Ki-yi! Ki-yi! Yippi-i-yip!" yelled the men.

"Bang! Bang! Bang!" exploded their revolvers.

"Oh, dear!" screamed Janet.

Teddy turned a little pale, but he did not make a sound.

"What is it?" asked Mrs. Martin, hugging Trouble and his sister closer to her. "Oh, what is it?"

"Don't be afraid!" laughed Uncle Frank. "Those are the cowboys making you welcome to Ring Rosy Ranch. That's their way of having fun!"

CHAPTER VII
BAD NEWS

On came the cowboys, yelling, shouting and shooting off their big revolvers which made noises like giant firecrackers. The men, some of whom wore big leather "pants," as Teddy said afterward, and some of whom had on trousers that seemed to be made from the fleece of sheep, swung their hats in the air. Some of them even stood up in their saddles, "just like circus riders!" as Janet sent word to Aunt Jo, who was spending the summer at Mt. Hope.

"Are they shooting real bullets, Uncle Frank?" asked Teddy, as soon as the noise died down a little and the cowboys were waving their hats to the Curlytops and the other visitors to Ring Rosy Ranch.

"Real bullets? Bless your heart, no!" exclaimed Mr. Barton. "Of course the cowboys sometimes have real bullets in their 'guns,' as they call their revolvers, but they don't shoot 'em for fun."

"What makes them shoot?" asked Janet.

"Well, sometimes it's to scare away bad men who might try to steal my cattle or horses, and again it's to scare the cattle themselves. You see," explained Uncle Frank, while the cowboys jumped from their horses and went to the bunk house to wash and get ready for supper, "a ranch is just like a big pasture that your Grandfather Martin has at Cherry Farm. Only my ranch is ever so much bigger than his pastures, even all of them put together. And there are very few fences around any of my fields, so the cattle or horses might easily stray off, or be taken.

"Because of that I have to hire men — cowboys they are called — to watch my cattle and horses, to see that they do not run away and that no white men or Indians come and run away with them.

"But sometimes the cattle take it into their heads to run away themselves. They get frightened — 'stampeded' we call it — and they don't care which way they run. Sometimes a prairie fire will make them run and again it may be bad men — thieves. The cowboys have to stop the cattle from running away, and they do it by firing revolvers in front of them. So it wouldn't do to have real bullets in their guns when the cowboys are firing that way. They use blank cartridges, just as they did now to salute you when they came in."

"Is that what they did?" asked Teddy. "Saluted us?"

"That's it. They just thought they'd have a little fun with you—see if they could scare you, maybe, because you're what they call a 'tenderfoot,' Teddy."

"Pooh, I wasn't afraid!" declared Teddy, perhaps forgetting a little. "I liked it. It was like the Fourth of July!"

"I didn't like it," said Janet, with a shake of her curly head. "And what's a soft-foot, Uncle Frank?"

"A soft-foot? Oh, ho! I see!" he laughed. "You mean a tenderfoot! Well, that's what the Western cowboys call anybody from the East—where you came from. It means, I guess, that their feet are tender because they walk so much and don't ride a horse the way cowboys do. You see out here we folks hardly ever walk. If we've only got what you might call a block to go we hop on a horse and ride. So we get out of the way of walking.

"Now you Eastern folk walk a good bit—that is when you aren't riding in street cars and in your automobiles, and I suppose that's why the cowboys call you tender-feet. You don't mind, though, do you, Teddy?"

"Nope," he said. "I like it. But I'm going to learn to ride a pony."

"So'm I!" exclaimed Janet.

"I wants a wide, too!" cried Trouble. "Can't I wide, Uncle Frank? We hasn't got Nicknack, but maybe you got a goat," and he looked up at his father's uncle.

"No, I haven't a goat," laughed Uncle Frank, "though there might be some sheep on some of the ranches here. But I guess ponies will suit you children better. When you Curlytops learn to ride you can take Trouble up on the saddle with you and give him a ride. He's too small to ride by himself yet."

"I should say he was, Uncle Frank!" cried Mrs. Martin. "Don't let him get on a horse!"

"I won't," promised Mr. Barton with a laugh. But Trouble said:

"I likes a pony! I wants a wide, Muz-zer!"

"You may ride with me when I learn," promised Janet.

"Dat nice," responded William.

Uncle Frank's wife, whom everyone called Aunt Millie, came out of the ranch house and welcomed the Curlytops and the others. She had not seen them for a number of years.

"My, how big the children are!" she cried as she looked at Janet and Teddy. "And here's one I've never seen," she went on, as she caught Trouble up in her arms and kissed him.

"Now come right in. Hop Sing has supper ready for you."

"Hop Sing!" laughed Mother Martin. "That sounds like a new record on the phonograph."

"It's the name of our Chinese cook," explained Aunt Millie, "and a very good one he is, too!"

"Are the cowboys coming in to eat with us?" asked Teddy, as they all went into the house, where the baggage had been carried by Uncle Frank and Daddy Martin.

"Oh, no. They eat by themselves in their own building. Not that we wouldn't have them, for they're nice boys, all of them, but they'd rather be by themselves."

"Do any Indians come in?" asked Janet, looking toward the door.

"Bless your heart, no!" exclaimed Aunt Millie. "We wouldn't want them, for they're dirty and not at all nice, though some of them do look like pictures when they wrap themselves around in a red blanket and stick feathers in their hair. We don't want any Indians. Now tell me about your trip."

"We were in a collision!" cried Janet.

"In the middle of the night," added Teddy.

"An' I mos' fell out of my bed!" put in Trouble.

Then, amid laughter, the story of the trip from the East was told. Meanwhile Hop Sing, the Chinese cook, cried out in his funny, squeaky voice that supper was getting cold.

"Well, well eat first and talk afterward," said Uncle Frank, as he led the way to the table. "Come on, folks. I expect you all have good appetites. That's what we're noted for at Ring Rosy Ranch."

"What's that?" asked Aunt Millie.

"Have you given Circle O a new name?"

"One of the Curlytops did," chuckled Uncle Frank. "They said my branding sign looked just like a ring-round-the-rosy, so I'm going to call the ranch that after this."

"It's a nice name," said Aunt Millie. "And now let me see you Curlytops — and Trouble, too — though his hair isn't frizzy like Ted's and Janet's — let me see you eat until you get as fat as a Ring Rosy yourselves. If you don't eat as much as you can of everything, Hop Sing will feel as though he was not a good cook."

The Curlytops were hungry enough to eat without having to be told to, and Hop Sing, looking into the dining-room now and then from where he was busy in the kitchen, smiled and nodded his head as he said to the maid.

"Lil' chillens eat velly good!"

"Indeed they do eat very good," said the maid, as she carried in more of the food which Hop Sing knew so well how to cook.

After supper the Curlytops and the others sat out on the broad porch of the ranch house. Off to one side were the other buildings, some where the farming tools were kept, for Uncle Frank raised some grain as well as cattle, and some where the cowboys lived, as well as others where they stabled their horses.

"I know what let's do," said Jan, when she and her brother had sat on the porch for some time, listening to the talk of the older folks, and feeling very happy that they were at Uncle Frank's ranch, where, they felt sure, they could have such good times.

"What can we do?" asked Teddy. Very often he let Jan plan some fun, and I might say that she got into trouble doing this as many times as her brother did. Jan was a regular boy, in some things. But then I suppose any girl is who has two nice brothers, even if one is little enough to be called "Baby."

"Let's go and take a walk," suggested Jan. "My legs feel funny yet from ridin' in the cars so much."

"Ri-ding!" yelled Teddy gleefully. "That's the time you forgot your g, Janet."

"Yes, I did," admitted the little girl. "But there's so much to look at here that it's easy to forget. My forgetter works easier than yours does, Ted."

"It does not!"

"It does, too!"

"It does not!"

"I—say—it—does!" and Janet was very positive.

"Now, now, children!" chided their mother. "That isn't nice. What are you disputing about now?"

"Jan says her forgetter's better'n mine!" cried Ted.

"And it is," insisted Janet. "I can forget lots easier than Ted."

"Well, forgetting isn't a very good thing to do," said Mr. Martin. "Remembering is better."

"Oh, that's what I meant!" said Jan. "I thought it was a forgetter. Anyhow mine's better'n Ted's!"

"Now don't start that again," warned Mother Martin, playfully shaking her finger at the two children. "Be nice now. Amuse yourselves in some quiet way. It will soon be time to go to bed. You must be tired. Be nice now."

"Come on, let's go for a walk," proposed Jan again, and Ted, now that the forget-memory dispute was over, was willing to be friendly and kind and go with his sister.

So while Trouble climbed up into his mother's lap, and the older folks were talking among themselves, the two Curlytops, not being noticed by the others, slipped off the porch and walked toward the ranch buildings, out near the corrals, or the fenced-in places, where the horses were kept.

There were too many horses to keep them all penned in, or fenced around, just as there are too many cattle on a cattle ranch. But the cowboys who do not want their horses which they ride to get too far away put them in a corral. This is just as good as a barn, except in cold weather.

"There's lots of things to see here," said Teddy, as he and his sister walked along.

"Yes," she agreed. "It's lots of fun. I'm glad I came."

"So'm I. Oh, look at the lots of ponies!" she cried, as she and Ted turned a corner of one of the ranch buildings and came in sight of a new corral. In it were a number of little horses, some of which hung their heads over the fence and watched the Curlytops approaching.

"I'd like to ride one," sighed Teddy wistfully.

"Oh, you mustn't!" cried Jan. "Uncle Frank wouldn't like it, nor mother or father, either. You have to ask first."

"Oh, I don't mean ride now," said Ted. "Anyhow, I haven't got a saddle."

"Can't you ride without a saddle?" asked Janet.

"Well, not very good I guess," Ted answered. "A horse's back has a bone in the middle of it, and that bumps you when you don't have a saddle."

"How do you know?" asked Janet.

"I know, 'cause once the milkman let me sit on his horse and I felt the bone in his back. It didn't feel good."

"Maybe the milkman's horse was awful bony."

"He was," admitted Ted. "But anyhow you've got to have a saddle to ride a horse, lessen you're a Indian and I'm not."

"Well, maybe after a while Uncle Frank'll give you a saddle," said Janet.

49

"Maybe," agreed her brother, "Oh, see how the ponies look at us!"

"And one's following us all around," added his sister. For the little horses had indeed all come to the side of the corral fence nearest the Curlytops, and were following along as the children walked.

"What do you s'pose they want?" asked Teddy.

"Maybe they're hungry," answered Janet.

"Let's pull some grass for 'em," suggested Teddy, and they did this, feeding it to the horses that stretched their necks over the top rail of the fence and chewed the green bunches as if they very much liked their fodder.

But after a while Jan and Ted tired of even this. And no wonder—there were so many horses, and they all seemed to like the grass so much that the children never could have pulled enough for all of them.

"Look at that one always pushing the others out of the way," said Janet, pointing to one pony, larger than the others, who was always first at the fence, and first to reach his nose toward the bunches of grass.

"And there's a little one that can't get any," said her brother. "I'd like to give him some, Jan."

"So would I. But how can we? Every time I hold out some grass to him the big horse takes it."

Teddy thought for a minute and then he said:

"I know what we can do to keep the big horse from getting it all."

"What?" asked Janet.

"We can both pull some grass. Then you go to one end of the fence, and hold out your bunch. The big horse will come to get it and push the others away, like he always does."

"But then the little pony won't get any," Janet said.

"Oh, yes, he will!" cried Teddy. "'Cause when you're feeding the big horse I'll run up and give the little horse my bunch. Then he'll have some all by himself."

And this the Curlytops did. When the big horse was chewing the grass Janet gave him, Ted held out some to the little horse at the other end of the corral, And he ate it, but only just in time, for the big pony saw what was going on and trotted up to shove the small animal out of the way. But it was too late.

Then Janet and Teddy walked on a little further, until Janet said it was growing late and they had better go back to the porch where the others were still talking.

Evening was coming on. The sun had set, but there was still a golden glow in the sky. Far off in one of the big fields a number of horses and cattle could be seen, and riding out near them were some of the cowboys who, after their supper, had gone out to see that all was well for the night.

"Is all this your land, Uncle Frank!" asked Teddy as he stood on the porch and looked over the fields.

"Yes, as far as you can see, and farther. If you Curlytops get lost, which I hope you won't, you'll have to go a good way to get off my ranch. But let me tell you now, not to go too far away from the house, unless your father or some of us grown folks are with you."

"Why?" asked Janet.

"Well, you might get lost, you know, and then—oh, well, don't go off by yourselves, that's all," and Uncle Frank turned to answer a question Daddy Martin asked him.

Ted and Janet wondered why they could not go off by themselves as they had done at Cherry Farm.

"Maybe it's because of the Indians," suggested Jan.

"Pooh, I'm not afraid of them," Teddy announced.

Just then one of the cowboys—later the children learned he was Jim Mason, the foreman—came walking up to the porch. He walked in a funny way, being more used to going along on a horse than on his own feet.

"Good evening, folks!" he said, taking off his hat and waving it toward the Curlytops and the others.

"Hello, Jim!" was Uncle Frank's greeting. "Everything all right?"

"No, it isn't, I'm sorry to say," answered the foreman. "I've got bad news for you, Mr. Barton!"

CHAPTER VIII

A QUEER NOISE

The Curlytops looked at the ranch foreman as he said this. Uncle Frank looked at him, too. The foreman stood twirling his big hat around in his hand. Teddy looked at the big revolver—"gun" the cowboys called it— which dangled from Jim Mason's belt.

"Bad news, is it?" asked Uncle Frank. "I'm sorry to hear that. I hope none of the boys is sick. Nobody been shot, has there, during the celebration?"

"Oh, no, the boys are all right," answered the foreman. "But it's bad news about some of your ponies—a lot of them you had out on grass over there," and he pointed to the west—just where Ted and Janet could not see.

"Bad news about the ponies?" repeated Uncle Frank. "Well, now, I'm sorry to hear that. Some of 'em sick?"

"Not as I know of," replied Jim. "But a lot of 'em have been taken away— stolen, I guess I'd better call it."

"A lot of my ponies stolen?" cried Uncle Frank, jumping up from his chair. "That is bad news! When did it happen? Why don't you get the cowboys together and chase after the men who took the ponies?"

"Well, I would have done that if I knew where to go," said the foreman. "But I didn't hear until a little while ago, when one of the cowboys I sent to see if the ponies were all right came in. He got there to find 'em all gone, so I came right over to tell you."

"Well, we'll have to see about this!" exclaimed Uncle Frank. "Who's the cowboy you sent to see about the ponies?"

"Henry Jensen. He just got in a little while ago, after a hard ride."

"And who does he think took the horses?"

"He said it looked as if the Indians had done it!" and at these words from the foreman Ted and Janet looked at one another with widely opened eyes.

"Indians?" said Uncle Frank. "Why, I didn't think any of them had come off their reservation."

"Some of 'em must have," the foreman went on. "They didn't have any ponies of their own, I guess, so they took yours and rode off on 'em."

"Well, this is too bad!" said Uncle Frank in a low voice. "I guess we'll have to get our boys together and chase after these Indians," he went on. "Yes, that's what I'll do. I've got to get back my ponies."

"Oh, can't I come?" cried Teddy, not understanding all that was going on, but enough to know that his uncle was going somewhere with the cowboys, and Teddy wanted to go, too.

"Oh, I'm afraid you couldn't come—Curlytop," said the foreman, giving Teddy the name almost everyone called him at first sight, and this was the first time Jim Mason had seen Teddy.

"No, you little folks must stay at home," added Uncle Frank.

"Are you really going after Indians?" Teddy wanted to know.

"Yes, to find out if they took any of my ponies. You see," went on Uncle Frank, speaking to Daddy and Mother Martin as well as to the Curlytops, "the Indians are kept on what is called a 'reservation' That is, the government gives them certain land for their own and they are told they must stay there, though once in a while some of them come off to sell blankets and bark-work at the railroad stations.

"And, sometimes, maybe once a year, a lot of the Indians get tired of staying on the reservation and some of them will get together and run off. Sometimes they ride away on their own horses, and again they may take some from the nearest ranch. I guess this time they took some of mine."

"And how will you catch them?" asked Mrs. Martin.

"Oh, we'll try to find out which way they went and then we'll follow after them until we catch them and get back the ponies."

"It's just like hide-and-go-seek, isn't it, Uncle Frank?" asked Janet.

"Yes, something like that But it takes longer."

"I wish I could go to hunt the Indians!" murmured Teddy.

"Why, The-o-dore Mar-tin!" exclaimed his mother. "I'm surprised at you!"

"Well, I would like to go," he said.

"Could I go if I knew how to ride a pony, Uncle Frank?"

"Well, I don't know. I'm afraid you're too little. But, speaking of riding a pony, to-morrow I'll have one of the cowboys start in to teach you and Janet to ride. Now I guess I'll have to go see this Henry Jensen and ask him about the Indians and my stolen ponies."

"I hope he gets them back," said Teddy to his sister.

"So do I," she agreed. "And I hope those Indians don't come here."

"Pooh! they're tame Indians!" exclaimed Teddy.

"They must be kind of wild when they steal ponies," Janet said.

A little later the Curlytops and Trouble went to bed, for they had been up early that day. They fell asleep almost at once, even though their bed was not moving along in a railroad train, as it had been the last three or four nights.

"Did Uncle Frank find his ponies?" asked Teddy the next morning at the breakfast table.

"No, Curlytop," answered Aunt Millie. "He and some of the cowboys have gone over to the field where the ponies were kept to see if they can get any news of them."

"Can we learn to ride a pony to-day?" asked Janet.

"As soon as Uncle Frank comes back," answered her father. "You and Ted and Trouble play around the house now as much as you like. When Uncle Frank comes back he'll see about getting a pony for you to ride."

"Come on!" called Ted to his sister after breakfast. "We'll have some fun."

"I come, too!" called Trouble. "I wants a wide! I wish we had Nicknack."

"It would be fun if we had our goat here, wouldn't it?" asked Janet of her brother.

"Yes, but I'd rather have a pony. I'm going to be a cowboy, and you can't be a cowboy and ride a goat."

"No, I s'pose not," said Janet. "But a goat isn't so high up as a pony, Ted, and if you fall off a goat's back you don't hurt yourself so much."

"I'm not going to fall off," declared Teddy.

The children wandered about among the ranch buildings, looking in the bunk house where the cowboys slept. There was only one person in there, and he was an old man to be called a "boy," thought Janet. But all men, whether young or old, who look after the cattle on a ranch, are called "cowboys" so age does not matter.

"Howdy," said this cowboy with a cheerful smile, as the Curlytops looked in at him. He was mending a broken strap to his saddle. "Where'd you get that curly hair?" he asked. "I lost some just like that. Wonder if you got mine?"

Janet hardly knew what to make of this, but Teddy said:

"No, sir. This is our hair. It's fast to our heads and we've had it a long time."

"It was always curly this way," added Janet.

"Oh, was it? Well, then it can't be mine," said the cowboy with a laugh. "Mine was curly only when I was a baby, and that was a good many years ago. Are you going to live here?"

"We're going to stay all summer," Janet said. "Do you live here?"

"Well, yes; as much as anywhere."

"Could you show us where the Indians are that took Uncle Frank's ponies?" Teddy demanded.

"Wish I could!" exclaimed the cowboy. "If I knew, I'd go after 'em myself and get the ponies back. I guess those Indians are pretty far away from here by now."

"Do they hide?" asked Teddy.

"Yes, they may hide away among the hills and wait for a chance to sell the ponies they stole from your uncle. But don't worry your curly heads about Indians. Have a good time here. It seems good to see little children around a place like this."

"Have you got a lasso?" asked Teddy.

"You mean my rope? Course I got one—every cowboy has," was the answer.

"I wish you'd lasso something," went on Teddy, who had once been to see a Wild West show.

"All right, I'll do a little rope work for you," said the cowboy, with a good-natured smile. "Just wait until I mend my saddle."

In a little while he came riding into the yard in front of the bunk house on a lively little pony. He made the animal race up and down and, while doing this, the cowboy swung his coiled rope, or lasso, about his head, and sent it in curling rings toward posts and benches, hauling the latter after him by winding the rope around the horn of his saddle after he had lassoed them.

"Say! that's fine!" cried Teddy with glistening eyes. "I'm going to learn how to lasso."

"I'll show you after a while," the cowboy offered. "You can't learn too young. But I must go now."

"Could I just have a little ride on your pony's back?" asked Teddy.

"To be sure you could," cried the cowboy. "Here you go!"

He leaped from the saddle and lifted Teddy up to it, while Janet and Trouble looked on in wonder. Then holding Ted to his seat by putting an arm around him, while he walked beside the pony and guided it, the cowboy gave the little fellow a ride, much to Teddy's delight.

"Hurray!" he called to Janet "I'm learning to be a cowboy!"

"That's right—you are!" laughed Daddy Martin, coming out just then. "How do you like it?"

"Dandy!" Teddy said. "Come on. Janet!"

"Yes, we ought to have let the ladies go first," said the cowboy. "But I didn't know whether the leetle gal cared for horses," he went on to Mr. Martin.

"I like horses," admitted Janet. "But maybe I'll fall off."

"I won't let you," the cowboy answered, as he lifted her to the saddle. Then he led the pony around with her on his back, and Janet liked it very much.

"I wants a wide, too!" cried Trouble.

"Hi! that's so! Mustn't forget you!" laughed the cowboy, and he held Baby William in the saddle, much to the delight of that little fellow.

"Now you mustn't bother any more," said Daddy Martin. "You children have had fun enough. You'll have more pony-back rides later."

"Yes, I'll have to go now," the cowboy said, and, leaping into the saddle, he rode away in a cloud of dust.

The Curlytops and Trouble wandered around among the ranch buildings. Daddy Martin, seeing that the children were all right, left them to themselves.

"I'se hungry," said Trouble, after a bit.

"So'm I," added Teddy. "Do you s'pose that funny Chinaman would give us a cookie, Jan?"

"Chinamen don't know how to make cookies."

"Well, maybe they know how to make something just as good. Let's go around to the cook house — that's what Aunt Millie calls it."

The cook house was easy to find, for from it came a number of good smells, and, as they neared it, the Curlytops saw the laughing face of the Chinese cook peering out at them.

"Lil' gal hungly — li' boy hungly?" asked Hop Sing in his funny talk.

"Got any cookies?" inquired Teddy.

"No glot clooklies — glot him clake," the Chinese answered.

"What does he say?" asked Janet of her brother.

"I guess he means cake," whispered Teddy, and that was just what Hop Sing did mean. He brought out some nice cake on a plate and Trouble and the Curlytops had as much as was good for them, if not quite all they wanted.

"Glood clake?" asked Hop Sing, when nothing but the crumbs were left—and not many of them.

"I guess he means was it good cake," then whispered Janet to her little brother.

"Yes, it was fine and good!" exclaimed Teddy. "Thank you."

"You mluch welclome—clome some mo'!" laughed Hop Sing, as the children moved away.

They spent the morning playing about the ranch near the house. They made a sea-saw from a board and a barrel, and played some of the games they had learned on Cherry Farm or while camping with Grandpa Martin. Then dinner time came, but Uncle Frank and the cowboys did not come back to it.

"Won't they be hungry?" asked Teddy.

"Oh, they took some bacon, coffee and other things with them," said Aunt Millie. "They often have to camp out for days at a time."

"Say, I wish I could do that!" cried Teddy.

"Wait until you get to be a cowboy," advised his father.

That afternoon Trouble went to lie down with his mother to have a nap, and Teddy and Janet wandered off by themselves, promising not to go too far away from the house.

But the day was so pleasant, and it was so nice to walk over the soft grass that, before they knew it, Teddy and Janet had wandered farther than they meant to. As the land was rolling—here hills and there hollows—they were soon out of sight of the ranch buildings, but they were not afraid, as they knew by going to a high part of the prairie they could see their way back home—or they thought they could. There were no woods around them, though there were trees and a little stream of water farther off.

Suddenly, as the Curlytops were walking along together, they came to a place where there were a lot of rocks piled up in a sort of shelter. Indeed one place looked as though it might be a cave. And as Teddy and Janet were looking at this they heard a strange noise, which came from among the rocks.

Both children stopped and stood perfectly still for a moment.

"Did you hear that?" asked Jan, clasping her brother's arm.

"Yes—I did," he answered.

"Did—did it sound like some one groaning?" she went on.

Teddy nodded his head to show that it had sounded that way to him. Just then the noise came again.

"Oh!" exclaimed Janet, starting to run. "Maybe it's an Indian! Oh, Teddy, come on!"

CHAPTER IX

THE SICK PONY

Teddy Martin did not run away as Jan started to leave the pile of rocks from which the queer sound had come. Instead he stood still and looked as hard as he could toward the hole among the stones—a hole that looked a little like the cave on Star Island, but not so large.

"Come on, Teddy!" begged Janet. "Please come!"

"I want to see what it is," he answered.

"Maybe it's something that—that'll bite you," suggested the little girl. "Come on!"

Just then the noise sounded again. It certainly was a groan.

"There!" exclaimed Janet. "I know it's an Indian, Ted! Maybe it's one of the kind that took Uncle Frank's ponies. Oh, please come!"

She had run on a little way from the pile of rocks, but now she stood still, waiting for Teddy to follow.

"Come on!" she begged.

Janet did not want to go alone.

"It can't be an Indian," said Teddy, looking around but still not seeing anything to make that strange sound.

"It could so be an Indian!" declared Janet.

"Well, maybe a sick Indian," Teddy admitted. "And if he's as sick as all that I'm not afraid of him! I'm going to see what it is."

"Oh, The-o-dore Mar-tin!" cried Janet, much as she sometimes heard her mother use her brother's name. "Don't you dare!"

"Why not?" asked Teddy, who tried to speak very bravely, though he really did not feel brave. But he was not going to show that before Janet, who was a girl. "Why can't I see what that is?"

"'Cause maybe—maybe it'll—bite you!" and as Janet said this she looked first at the rocks and then over her shoulder, as though something might come up behind her when she least expected it.

"Pooh! I'm not afraid!" declared Teddy.

"Anyhow, if it does bite me it's got to come out of the rocks first."

"Well, maybe it will come out."

"If it does I can see it and run!" went on the little boy.

"Would you run and leave me all alone?" asked Janet.

"Nope! Course I wouldn't do that," Teddy declared. "I'd run and I'd help you run. But I don't guess anything'll bite me. Anyhow, Indians don't bite."

"How do you know?" asked Janet. "Some Indians are wild. I heard Uncle Frank say so, and wild things bite!"

"But not Indians," insisted Teddy. "A Indian's mouth, even if he is wild, is just like ours, and it isn't big enough to bite. You've got to have an awful big mouth to bite."

"Henry Watson bit you once, I heard mother say so," declared Janet, as she and her brother still stood by the rocks and listened again for the funny sound to come from the stones. But there was silence.

"Well, Henry Watson's got an awful big mouth," remarked Teddy. "Maybe he's wild, and that's the reason."

"He couldn't be an Indian, could he?" Janet went on.

"Course not!" declared her brother. "He's a boy, same as I am, only his mouth's bigger. That's why he bit me. I 'member it now."

"Did it hurt?" asked Janet.

"Yep," answered her brother. "But I'm going in there and see what that noise was. It won't hurt me."

Teddy began to feel that Janet was asking so many questions in order that he might forget all about what he intended to do. And he surely did want to see what was in among the rocks.

Once more he went closer to them, and then the noise sounded more loudly than before. It came so suddenly that Teddy and Janet jumped back, and there was no doubt but what they were both frightened.

"Oh, I'm not going to stay here another minute!" cried Janet. "Come on, Ted, let's go home!"

"No, wait just a little!" he begged. "I'll go in and come right out again—that is if it's anything that bites. If it isn't you can come in with me."

"No, I'm not going to do that!" and Janet shook her head very decidedly to say "no!" Once more she looked over her shoulder.

"Well, you don't have to come in," Teddy said. "I'll go alone. I'm not scared."

Just then Janet looked across the fields, and she saw a man riding along on a pony.

"Oh, Teddy!" she called to her brother. "Here's a man! We can get him to go in and see what it is."

Teddy looked to where his sister pointed. Surely enough, there was a man going along. He was quite a distance off, but the Curlytops did not mind that. They were fond of walking.

"Holler at him!" advised Janet. "He'll hear us and come to help us find out what's in here."

Teddy raised his voice in the best shout he knew how to give. He had strong lungs and was one of the loudest-shouting boys among his chums.

"Hey, Mister! Come over here!" cried Teddy.

But the man kept on as if he had not heard, as indeed he had not. For on the prairies the air is so clear that people and things look much nearer than they really are. So, though the man seemed to be only a little distance away, he was more than a mile off, and you know it is quite hard to call so as to be heard a mile away; especially if you are a little boy.

Still Teddy called again, and when he had done this two or three times, and Jan had helped him, the two calling in a sort of duet, Teddy said:

"He can't hear us."

"Maybe he's deaf, like Aunt Judy," said Janet, speaking of an elderly woman in the town in which they lived.

"Well, if he is, he can't hear us," said Teddy; "so he won't come to us. I'm going in anyhow."

"No, don't," begged Janet, who did not want her brother to go into danger. "If he can't hear us, Teddy, we must go nearer. We can walk to meet him."

Teddy thought this over a minute.

"Yes," he agreed, "we can do that. But he's a good way off."

"He's coming this way," Janet said, and it did look as though the man had turned his horse toward the children, who stood near the pile of rocks from which the queer noises came.

"Come on!" decided Ted, and, taking Janet's hand, he and she walked toward the man on the horse.

For some little time the two Curlytops tramped over the green, grassy prairies. They kept their eyes on the man, now and then looking back toward the rocks, for they did not want to lose sight either of them or of the horseman.

"I'm going to holler again," said Teddy. "Maybe he can hear me now. We're nearer."

So he stopped, and putting his hands to his mouth, as he had seen Uncle Frank do when he wanted to call to a cowboy who was down at a distant corral, the little boy called:

"Hi there, Mr. Man! Come here, please!"

But the man on the horse gave no sign that he had heard. As a matter of fact, he had not, being too far away, and the wind was blowing from him toward Teddy and Jan. If the wind had been blowing the other way it might have carried the voices of the children toward the man. But it did not.

Then Teddy made a discovery. He stopped, and, shading his eyes with his hands, said:

"Jan, that man's going away from us 'stid of coming toward us. He's getting littler all the while. And if he was coming to us he'd get bigger."

"Yes, I guess he would," admitted the little girl. "He is going away, Teddy. Oh, dear! Now he can't help us!"

Without a word Teddy started back toward the rocks, and his sister followed. He was close to them when Janet spoke again.

"What are you going to do?" she asked.

"I'm going in there and see what that noise was," Teddy replied.

"Oh, you mustn't!" she cried, hoping to turn him away. But Teddy answered:

"Yes, I am, too! I'm going to see what it is!"

"I'm not!" cried Janet. "I'm going home. You'd better come with me!"

But, though she turned away and went a short distance from the rocks in the direction she thought the ranch house of Ring Rosy Ranch should be, she very soon stopped. She did not like going on alone. She looked back at Ted.

Teddy had walked a little way toward the hole in the rocks. Now he called to his sister.

"The noise comes from in here," he said. "It's in this little cave."

"Are you going in?" asked Janet, trying to pretend she was not afraid.

"I want to see what made that noise," declared Teddy. Since he and his sister had gone camping with Grandpa Martin they were braver than they used to be. Of course, Ted, being a year older than his sister, was a little bolder than she was.

Janet, not feeling that she ought to run on home and leave Teddy there and yet not feeling brave enough to go close to the cave among the rocks with him, hardly knew what to do. She walked back a little way and then, suddenly, the noise came, more loudly than at first.

"Oh, there it goes again!" cried Janet, once more running back.

"I heard it," Teddy said. "It didn't war-whoop like an Indian."

"If he's sick he couldn't," explained Janet.

"And if he's sick he can't hurt us," went on Teddy. "I'm going to holler at him and see what he wants."

"You'd better come back and tell daddy or Uncle Frank," suggested Janet.

Teddy rather thought so himself, but he did not like to give up once he had started anything. He felt it would be a fine thing if he, all alone, could find one of the Indians.

"And maybe it is one of those who took Uncle Frank's ponies," thought Teddy to himself.

Again the groan sounded, this time not quite so loud, and after it had died away Teddy called:

"Who's in there? What's the matter with you?"

No answer came to this. Then Ted added:

"If you don't come out I'm going to tell my uncle on you. He owns this ranch. Come on out! Who are you?"

This time there came a different sound. It was one that the Curlytops knew well, having heard it before.

"That's a horse whinnying!" cried Teddy.

"Or a pony," added Janet. "Yes, it did sound like that. Oh, Ted, maybe it's a poor horse in there and he can't get out!" she went on.

Again came the whinny of a horse or a pony. There was no mistake about it this time.

"Come on!" cried Teddy. "We've got to get him out, Janet. He's one of Uncle Frank's cow ponies and he's hurt in that cave. We've got to get him out!"

"But how can you?" Janet inquired. "It's an awful little cave, and I don't believe a pony could get in there."

"A little pony could," said Teddy.

Janet looked at the cave. She remembered that she had seen some quite small ponies, not only on Ring Rosy Ranch but elsewhere. The cave would be large enough for one of them.

"I'm going in," said Teddy, as he stood at the mouth of the hole among the piled-up rocks.

"He might kick you," warned Janet.

"If he's sick enough to groan that way he can't kick very hard," replied Teddy. "Anyhow, I'll keep out of the way of his feet. That's all you've got to do, Uncle Frank says, when you go around a strange horse. When he gets to know you he won't kick."

"Well, you'd better be careful," warned Janet again.

"Don't you want to come in?" Teddy asked his sister.

"I—I guess not," she answered. "I'll watch you here. Oh, maybe if it's a pony we can have him for ours, Teddy!" she exclaimed.

"Maybe," he agreed. "I'm going to see what it is."

Slowly he walked to the dark place amid the rocks. The whinnyings and groanings sounded plainer to him than to Janet, and Teddy was sure they came from a horse or a pony. As yet, though, he could see nothing.

Then, as the little boy stepped out of the glaring sun into the shadow cast by the rocks, he began to see better. And in a little while his eyes became used to the gloom.

Then he could see, lying down on the dirt floor of the cave amid the rocks, the form of a pony. The animal raised its head as Teddy came in and gave a sort of whinnying call, followed by a groan.

"Poor pony!" called Ted. "Are you hurt? I'm so sorry! I'll go get a doctor for you!"

"Who are you talking to?" asked Janet.

She had drawn nearer the cave.

"There's a sick pony in here all right," Teddy told his sister. "Come on in and look."

"I—I don't b'lieve I want to."

"Pooh! he can't hurt you! He's sick!" cried Teddy.

So, after waiting a half minute, Janet went in. In a little while she, too, could see the pony lying down in the cave.

"Oh, the poor thing!" she cried. "Teddy, we've got to help him!"

"Course we have," he said. "We've got to go for a doctor."

"And get him a drink," added Janet. "When anybody's sick—a pony or anybody—they want a drink. Let's find some water, Teddy. We can bring it to him in our hats!"

Then, leaving the sick pony in the cave, the Curlytops ran out to look for water.

CHAPTER X
A SURPRISED DOCTOR

Water is not very plentiful on the prairies. In fact, it is so scarce that often men and horses get very thirsty. But the Curlytops were lucky in finding a spring among the rocks on Ring Rosy Ranch. It was not a very large spring, and it was well hidden among the big stones, which, is, perhaps, why it was not visited by many of the ponies and cattle. They come in large numbers to every water-hole they can find.

Jan and Ted, having come out of the dark cave-like hole, where the poor, sick pony lay, began their search for water, and, as I have said, they were lucky in finding some.

It was Jan who discovered it. As the Curlytops were running about among the rocks the little girl stopped suddenly and called:

"Hark, Teddy!"

"What is it?" he asked.

"I hear water dripping," she answered. "It's over this way."

She went straight to the spring, following the sound of the dripping water, and found where it bubbled up in a split in the rock. The water fell into a little hollow, rocky basin and there was enough for Ted and his sister to fill their hats. First they each took a drink themselves, though, for the day was warm.

Their hats were of felt, and would hold water quite well. And as the hats were old ones, which had been worn in the rain more than once, dipping them into the spring would not hurt them.

"I guess the pony'll be awful glad to get a drink," said Jan to her brother.

"I guess he will," he answered, as he walked along looking carefully where he put down his feet, for he did not want to stumble and spill the water in his hat.

"Look out!" exclaimed Janet, as her brother came too close to her. "If you bump against me and make my arm jiggle you'll spill my hatful."

"I'll be careful," said Teddy.

They spilled some of the water, for their hats were not as good as pails in which to carry the pony's drink. But they managed to get to the cave with most of it.

"You can give him the first drink," said Teddy to his sister. "I found him, and he's my pony, but you can give him the first drink."

Janet felt that this was kind on Teddy's part, but still she did not quite like what he said about the pony.

"Is he going to be all yours?" she asked.

"Well, didn't I find him?"

"Yes, but when I found a penny once and bought a lollypop, I gave you half of it."

"Yes, you did," admitted Teddy, thinking of that time. "But I can't give you half the pony, can I?"

"No, I guess not. But you could let me ride on him."

"Oh, I'll do that!" exclaimed Teddy quickly. He was thinking it would be a hard matter to divide a live pony in half.

"Course I'll let you ride on him!" he went on. "We'll get Uncle Frank to let us have a saddle and some of the cowboys can teach us to ride. And I'll let you feed and water him as much as you like. I'm going to call him Clipclap."

"That's a funny name," remarked Janet.

"It's how his feet sound when he runs," explained Teddy. "Don't you know—clip-clap, clip-clap!" and he imitated the sound of a pony as best he could.

"Oh, yes!" exclaimed Janet. "They do go that way."

"I haven't heard this one run," added Teddy, "'cause he's sick and he can't gallop. But I guess his feet would make that sound, so I'm going to call him Clipclap."

"It's a nice name," agreed Janet. "But I guess we better give him a drink now. He must be awful thirsty."

"He is," said Teddy. "Hear him groan?"

The pony was again making a noise that did sound like a groan. He must be in pain the children thought.

"Go on—give him your drink, Janet," urged Teddy. "Then I'll give him mine."

Janet was afraid no longer. She went into the cave ahead of her brother, and as the pony was lying down Janet had to kneel in front of him with her hat full of water—no, it was not full, for some had spilled out, but there was still a little in it.

The pony smelled the water when Janet was yet a little way from him, and raised his head and part of his body by his forefeet. Though clear, cold water has no smell to us, animals can smell it sometimes a long way off, and can find their way to it when their masters would not know where to go for a drink.

"Oh, see how glad he is to get it!" exclaimed Janet, as the pony eagerly sucked up from her hat the water in it. The little animal drank very fast, as if he had been without water a long while.

"Now give him yours, Teddy," Janet called to her brother, and he kneeled down and let the pony drink from his hat.

"I guess he wants more," Janet said as the sick animal sucked up the last drops from Teddy's hat. "It wasn't very much."

"We'll get more!" Teddy decided. "Then we'll go for a doctor."

"Where'll we find one?" Janet asked.

"I know where to find him," Teddy answered.

Once more the children went back to the spring and again they filled their soft hats. And once more the pony greedily drank up the last drops of water. As he finished that in Ted's hat he dropped back again and stretched out as if very tired.

"Oh, I hope he doesn't die!" exclaimed Janet.

"So do I," added her brother. "I'd like to have a ride on him when he gets well. Come on, we'll go find the doctor."

Shaking the water drops from their hats the Curlytops put them on and went out of the cave into the sunlight. Led by Teddy, Janet followed to the top of the pile of rocks.

"Do you see that white house over there?" asked Teddy, pointing to one down the road that led past the buildings of Ring Rosy Ranch.

"Yes, I see it," Janet answered.

"That's the place where the doctor lives," went on Ted.

"How do you know?" demanded Janet.

"'Cause I heard Uncle Frank say so. Mother asked where a doctor lived, and Uncle Frank showed her that white house. I was on the porch and I heard him. He said if ever we needed a doctor we only had to go there and Doctor Bond would come right away. He's the only doctor around here."

"Then we'd better get him for our pony Clipclap!" exclaimed Janet. "Come on, Teddy."

"If we had our goat-wagon we could ride," said the little boy, as they walked along over the prairie together. "But I guess we've got to walk now."

"Is it very far?" asked Janet.

"No, not very far. I've never been there, but you can easy see it."

Truly enough the white house of Doctor Bond was in plain sight, but on the prairies the air is so clear that distant houses look nearer than they really are.

So, though Ted and Janet thought they would be at the doctor's in about ten minutes, they were really half an hour in reaching the place. They saw the doctor's brass sign on his house.

"I hope he's in," said Teddy.

As it happened Doctor Bond was in, and he came to the door himself when Teddy rang the bell, Mrs. Bond being out in the chicken part of the yard.

"Well, children, what can I do for you?" asked Doctor Bond with a pleasant smile, as he saw the Curlytops on his porch.

"If you please," began Teddy, "will you come and cure Clipclap?"

"Will I come and cure him? Well, I will do my best. I can't be sure I'll cure him, though, until I know what the matter is. What seems to be the trouble?"

"He's awful sick," said Janet, "and he groans awful."

"Hum! He must have some pain then."

"We gave him some cold water," added Teddy.

"Yes? Well, maybe that was a good thing and maybe it wasn't. I can't tell until I see him. Who did you say it was?"

"Clipclap," replied Teddy.

"Your little brother?"

"No, sir. He's a pony and he's in a cave!" exclaimed Teddy.

"What? A pony?" cried the surprised doctor. "In a cave?"

"Yes," went on Janet. "We gave him water in our hats, and he's going to be Ted's and mine 'cause Ted found him. But will you please come and cure him so we can have a ride on him? Don't let him die."

"Well," exclaimed Doctor Bond, smiling in a puzzled way at the children, "I don't believe I can come. I don't know anything about curing sick ponies. You need a horse doctor for that."

Ted and Janet looked at one another, not knowing what to say.

CHAPTER XI
TROUBLE MAKES A LASSO

Doctor Bond must have seen how disappointed Teddy and Janet were, for he spoke very kindly as he asked:

"Who are you, and where are you from? Tell me about this sick pony with the funny name."

"He is Clipclap," answered Teddy, giving the name he had picked out for his new pet. "And we are the Curlytops."

"Yes, I can see that all right," laughed the doctor with a look at the crisp hair of the little boy and girl. "But where do you live?"

"At Uncle Frank's ranch," Janet answered.

"You mean Mr. Frank Barton, of the Circle O?" the doctor inquired.

"Yes, only we call it the Ring Rosy Ranch now, and so does he," explained Teddy.

"The Ring Rosy Ranch, is it? Well, I don't know but what that is a good name for it. Now tell me about yourselves and this pony."

This Teddy and Janet did by turns, relating how they had come out West from Cresco, and what good times they were having. They even told about having gone to Cherry Farm, about camping with Grandpa Martin and about being snowed in.

"Well, you have had some nice adventures!" exclaimed Doctor Bond. "Now about this sick — "

"Is some one ill?" enquired Mrs. Bond, coming in from the chicken yard just then, in time to hear her husband's last words, "Who is it?"

On the Western prairies when one neighbor hears of another's illness he or she wants to help in every way there is. So Mrs. Bond, hearing that some one was ill, wanted to do her share.

"It's a pony," her husband said with a smile.

"A pony!" she exclaimed.

"Yes, these Curlytop children found one in the cave among the rocks. It's on Circle O Ranch—I should say Ring Rosy," and the doctor gave Uncle Frank's place the new name. "These are Mr. Barton's nephew's children," he went on, for Ted and Janet had told the doctor that it was their father's uncle, and not theirs, at whose home they were visiting. Though, as a matter of fact, Ted and Janet thought Uncle Frank was as much theirs as he was their father's and, very likely, Uncle Frank thought so himself.

"Can't you come and cure the sick pony?" asked Teddy.

"He's groaning awful hard," went on Janet.

"Well, my dear Curlytops," said Doctor Bond with a smile, "I'd like to come, but, as I said, I don't know anything about curing sick horses or animals. I never studied that. It takes a doctor who knows about them to give them the right kind of medicine."

"I thought all medicine was alike," said Teddy. "What our doctor gives us is always bitter."

"Well, all medicine isn't bitter," laughed Doctor Bond, "though some very good kinds are. However, I wouldn't know whether to give this Clipclap pony bitter or sweet medicine."

"Maybe you could ask one of the cowboys," said Janet. "I heard Mr. Mason—Jim, Uncle Frank calls him—telling how he cured a sick horse once."

"Oh, yes, your uncle's foreman, Jim Mason, knows a lot about horses," said Doctor Bond.

"Then why don't you go with the children and get Jim to help you find out what the matter is with their pony?" suggested Mrs. Bond. "There isn't a regular veterinary around here, and they don't want to see their pet suffer. Go along with them."

"I believe I will," said Doctor Bond. "I could perhaps tell what's the matter with the pony, and if I've got any medicine that might cure it, Jim would know how to give it—I wouldn't."

"We just found the pony in the cave," explained Teddy. "We were taking a walk and we heard him groan."

"Oh, I see," said Mrs. Bond. "Well, I hope the doctor can make him well for you," she went on, as her husband hurried back into the house to get ready for the trip.

He had a small automobile, and in this he and the children were soon hurrying along the road toward Ring Rosy Ranch. It was decided to go there first instead of to the cave where the pony was.

"We'll get Jim Mason and take him back with us," said the doctor.

Uncle Frank and his cowboys had come back from looking after the lost ponies, but had not found them. He, as well as Mr. and Mrs. Martin, were very much surprised when the Curlytops came riding up to the ranch in Doctor Bond's automobile.

"Well, where in the world have you been?" cried Mother Martin. "We were just beginning to get worried about you children. Where were you?"

"We found a pony!" cried Janet.

"And he's sick!" added Teddy.

"And his name is Clipclap!" exclaimed the little girl.

"And he's mine but Janet can have half of him, and we got him water in our hats," came from Teddy.

"And we got the doctor, too!" went on his sister.

"Well, I should say you'd put in quite a busy day," chuckled Uncle Frank. "Now let's hear more about it."

So the Curlytops told, and Doctor Bond said, even if he was not a horse doctor, he'd go out and look at the pony in the cave, if the ranch foreman would come with him.

"Of course I'll come!" cried Jim Mason. "I wouldn't want to see any pony suffer. And I've doctored quite a few of 'em, even if I don't know much about medicine. Come on, Curlytops!"

Jim Mason jumped on his own swift pony, saying he could make as good time over the rough prairie as Doctor Bond could in his automobile. The Curlytops rode in the machine with the physician. Uncle Frank and Daddy Martin went along, for they, too, were interested in the sick pony.

It did not take long to get to the cave amid the rocks. Jim Mason's horse reached there ahead of the automobile, and the foreman had gone into the cave and come out again by the time the Curlytops were getting out of the machine.

"Well, he's a pretty sick pony all right," said the foreman of the cowboys of Ring Rosy Ranch.

"Can you make him better?" asked Teddy anxiously.

"I don't know whether we can or not. It all depends on what sort of medicine the doctor has for curing poison."

"Has the pony been poisoned?" asked Uncle Frank.

"Looks that way," replied the foreman. "I guess he must have drunk some water that had a bit of poisoned meat in it. You see," he went on to the doctor, Mr. Martin and the children, "we have a lot of wolves and other pesky animals around here. They're too tricky to catch in traps or shoot, so we poison 'em by putting a white powder in some meat. Sometimes the wolves will drag a piece of the poisoned meat to a spring of water, and they must have done it this time. Then the pony drank the water and it made him sick."

"Will he die?" asked Janet.

"Well, I'll do my best to save him," said Doctor Bond, opening the black case of medicines he carried. "But how can you give medicine to a horse, Jim? You can't put it on his tongue, can you?"

"No, but I've got a long-necked bottle on purpose for that, and it's easy to pour it out of that bottle down a pony's throat. You mix up the dose, Doc, and I'll give it to the little animal."

This was done, but the Curlytops were not allowed in the cave when the men were working over the pony. But, in a little while, the foreman and Doctor Bond came out.

"Well, I guess your pony will get better," said the physician. "Jim gave him the medicine that will get the poison out of him, and in a day or so he'll be able to walk. But you'll have to leave him in the cave until then."

"Can't we take him home?" Teddy cried.

"Oh, no!" exclaimed the foreman. "But I'll send one of the men over with some straw to make him a soft bed, and we'll see that he has water to drink. He won't want anything to eat until he gets better. The doctor will come to see him to-morrow. Won't you?" he went on to Doctor Bond.

"Indeed I will!" promised the doctor, for he had taken a great liking to the Curlytops.

"Whose pony is it?" asked Daddy Martin.

"It's mine!" exclaimed Teddy quickly. "Mine and Jan's. We found him and his name's Clipclap."

"Well, that's a good name for a pony," said his father. "But still I don't know that you can claim every pony you find. This one may belong to Uncle Frank."

"No, it isn't one of my brand," said the owner of Ring Rosy Ranch. "It's a strange pony that must have wandered into this cave after he found he was poisoned. I reckon the poor thing thought he'd die in there, and maybe he would if the children hadn't found him."

"He couldn't have lived much longer without attention," said Doctor Bond.

"Then did we save his life?" asked Teddy.

"You did, by getting the doctor in time," answered his father.

"Then can't he be our pony?" asked the little boy.

"Yes, I guess he can," answered Uncle Frank. "If nobody comes to claim him you children may have him. And if anyone does come after him I'll give you another. I was going to give you each a pony, anyhow, as soon as you got used to the ranch, and I'll do it. If Ted wants to keep Clipclap, as he calls him, I'll give Janet another."

"Oh, won't I just love him!" cried the little girl.

"And I'll love Clipclap!" said Teddy.

There was nothing more that could be done just then for the sick pony, so the Curlytops and the others left him in the cave. The children were glad he did not groan any more. A little later Jim Mason sent one of the cowboys with some clean straw to make a bed for the little horse, and a pail of the cool, spring water was put where the animal could reach it.

For two days the pony stayed in the cave, and then Doctor Bond said he was much better and could be led to the ranch. Uncle Frank took Ted and Janet out to the rocks to bring back their pet, but he had to walk very slowly, for he was still weak from the poison.

"And hell have to stay in the stable for a week or so," said Jim Mason when Clipclap was safely at the ranch. "After that he will be strong enough to ride. While you Curlytops are waiting I'll give you a few riding lessons."

"And will you show me how to lasso?" begged Teddy.

"Yes, of course. You'll never be a cowboy, as you say you're going to be, unless you can use a rope. I'll show you."

So the children's lessons began. Uncle Frank picked out a gentle pony for them on which to learn how to ride, and this pony was to be Jan's. She named him Star Face, for he had a white mark, like a star, on his forehead.

On this pony Jan and Ted took turns riding until they learned to sit in the saddle alone and let the pony trot along. Of course he did not go very fast at first.

"And I want to learn to lasso when I'm on his back," said Teddy.

"You'd first better learn to twirl the rope while you're on the ground," said Jim Mason, and then the foreman began giving the little boy some simple lessons in this, using a small rope, for Teddy could not handle the big ones the cowboys used.

In a few days Teddy could fling the coils of his rope and make them settle over a post. Of course he had to stand quite close, but even the cowboys, when they learned, had to do that the foreman said.

"Well, what are you going to do now?" Teddy's father asked the little boy one day, as he started out from the house with a small coil of rope on one arm, as he had seen the cowboys carry their lariats. "What are you going to do, Ted?"

"Oh, I'm going to lasso some more," was the answer.

"Why don't you try something else besides a post?" asked one of Uncle Frank's men, as he, too, noticed Teddy. "Throwing a rope over a post is all right to start, but if you want to be a real cowboy you'll have to learn to lasso something that's running on its four legs. That's what most of our lassoing is—roping ponies or steers, and they don't very often stand still for you, the way the post does."

"Yes," agreed Ted, "I guess so. I'll learn to lasso something that runs."

His father paid little more attention to the boy, except to notice that he went out into the yard, where he was seen, for a time, tossing the coils of rope over the post. Then Jan came along, and, as soon as he saw her, Teddy asked:

"Jan, will you do something for me?"

"What?" she inquired, not being too ready to make any promises. Sometimes Teddy got her to say she would do things, and then, when he had her promise, he would tell her something she did not at all want to do. So Jan had learned to be careful.

"What do you want to do, Teddy?" she asked.

"Play cowboy," he answered.

"Girls can't be cowboys," Janet said.

"Well, I don't want you to be one," went on Teddy. "I'll be the cowboy."

"Then what'll I be?" asked Jan. "That won't be any fun, for you to do that and me do nothing!"

"Oh, I've got something for you to do," said Teddy, and he was quite serious over it. "You see, Jan, I've got to learn to lasso something that moves. The post won't move, but you can run."

"Do you mean run and play tag?" Jan asked.

Teddy shook his head.

"You make believe you're a wild cow or a pony," he explained, "and you run along in front of me. Then I'll throw my rope around your head, or around your legs, and I'll pull on it and you—"

"Yes, and I'll fall down and get all dirt!" finished Jan. "Ho! I don't call that any fun for me!"

"Well, I won't lasso you very hard," promised Ted; "and I've got to learn to throw my rope at something that moves, the cowboys say, else I can't ever be a real wild-wester. Go on, Jan! Run along and let me lasso you!"

Jan did not want to, but Teddy teased her so hard that she finally gave in and said she would play she was a pony for a little while. Teddy wanted her to be a wild steer, but she said ponies could run faster than the cattle, and Jan was a good runner.

"And if I run fast it will be harder for you to lasso me," she said, "and that's good practice for you, same as it is good for me when I practice my music scales fast, only I don't do it very much."

"Well, you run along and I'll lasso you," said Teddy. "Only we'd better go around to the back of the house. Maybe they wouldn't like to see me doing it."

"Who; the cowboys?" asked his sister.

"No, father and mother," replied Teddy. "I don't guess they'd want me to play this game, but I won't hurt you. Come on."

The little boy and girl—Teddy carrying his small lasso—went out to a field not far from the house, and there they played cowboy. As they had planned, Teddy was the cowboy and Janet the wild pony, and she ran around until she was tired. Teddy ran after her, now and then throwing the coil of rope at her.

Sometimes the lasso settled over her head, and then the little boy would pull it tight, but he was careful not to pull too hard for fear he might hurt Jan. Once the rope went around her legs, and that time Teddy gave a sudden yank.

"Oh, I'm falling!" cried Jan, and she went down in a heap.

"That's fine!" cried Teddy. "That's regular wild-wester cowboy! Do it again, Jan!"

"No! It hurts!" objected the little girl. "You pulled me so hard I fell down."

"I didn't mean to," said Teddy. "But I can lasso good, can't I?"

"Yes; pretty good," his sister agreed. "But you can't lasso me any more. I don't want to play. I'm going to the house."

"Did I hurt you much?" Teddy asked.

"Well, not such an awful lot," admitted Jan. "I fell on some soft grass, though, or you would have. Anyhow, I'm going in."

Teddy looked a little sad for a minute, and then he cried:

"Oh, I know what I can do! You stay and watch me, Jan."

"What are you going to do?" she asked.

"You'll see," he answered "Here, you hold my lasso a minute."

Teddy ran off across the field, and when he came back to where his sister was still holding the coil of rope the Curlytop boy was leading by a rope a little calf, one of several that were kept in the stable and fed milk from a pail.

"What are you going to do, Teddy Martin?" asked the little girl.

"I'm going to play he's a wild steer," answered Teddy.

"Oh, The-o-dore Mar-tin!" cried Janet, much as her mother might have done. "You're not going to lasso him, are you?"

"I am — if I can," and Teddy spoke slowly. He was not quite sure he could.

The calf came along easily enough, for Teddy had petted it and fed it several times.

"He's awful nice," said Janet. "You won't hurt him, will you?"

"Course not!" cried Teddy. "I'll only lasso him a little. Now you come and hold him by the rope that's on his neck, Jan. And when I tell you to let go, why, you let go. Then he'll run and I can lasso him. I've got to lasso something that's running, else it isn't real wild-wester."

Jan was ready enough to play this game. She took hold of the calf's rope, and Teddy got his lasso ready. But just as the little fellow was about to tell his sister to let the calf loose, along came Uncle Frank and he saw what was going on.

"Oh, my, Teddy!" cried the ranchman. "You mustn't do that, Curlytop! The little calf might fall and break a leg. Wait until you get bigger before you try to lasso anything that's alive. Come on, we'll have other fun than this. I'm going to drive into town and you Curly tops can come with me."

So the calf was put back in the stable, and Teddy gave up lassoing for that day. He and Jan had fun riding to town with Uncle Frank, who bought them some sticks of peppermint candy.

Baby William had his own fun on the ranch. His mother took care of him most of the time, leaving Janet and Teddy to do as they pleased. She wanted them to learn to ride, and she knew they could not do it and take care of their little brother.

But Trouble had his own ways of having fun. He often watched Teddy throwing the lasso, and one afternoon, when Ted had finished with his rope and left it lying on a bench near the house, Trouble picked up the noose.

"Me lasso, too," he said to himself.

Just what he did no one knew, but not long after Teddy had laid aside the lariat, as the lasso is sometimes called, loud squawks, crowings and cackles from the chicken yard were heard.

"What in the world can be the matter with my hens?" cried Aunt Millie.

Ted and Janet ran out to see. What they saw made them want to laugh, but they did not like to do it.

CHAPTER XII

THE BUCKING BRONCO

With a small rope around the neck of the crowing rooster—which could not crow as loudly as it had before, because it was nearly choked—Trouble was dragging the fowl along after him as he ran across the yard.

"Trouble! Trouble!" cried Aunt Millie. "What are you doing?"

"Playin' cowboy!" was his answer. "I lasso rooster wif my rope, like Teddy catches post."

"Oh, you mustn't do that!" cried Aunt Millie, as she ran after the small boy and the dragging rooster.

"Cock-a doodle-do!" crowed the rooster, or, rather, it tried to crow that way, but it would get only about half of it out and then Trouble would pull the rope tight about the fowl's neck and the crow would be shut off suddenly.

"Gid-dap, pony!" cried Baby William, trotting along on his short, fat legs, making-believe, as he often did, that he was riding horseback. "Gid-dap! I lasso a rooster, I did!"

"Yes, and you'll kill the poor thing if you're not careful," panted Aunt Millie, as she raced after the little fellow and caught him. Then she gently pulled the rooster to her by means of the rope, and took it off the fowl's neck.

The rooster was bedraggled from having been dragged through the dust and the dirt, and it was so dizzy from having been whirled around by Trouble that it could hardly stand up.

Aunt Millie smoothed out its feathers and got it some water. The rooster drank a little and seemed to feel better. Then it ran off to join the other roosters and the cackling hens that had been watching what Trouble did, doubtless wondering what had gotten into the lassoed rooster to make it run around the way it did on the end of a rope. But it was Baby William who made all the trouble.

"You must never do that again," said Mrs. Martin when she came out of the ranch house and heard what her little boy had done. "That was very wrong, William, to lasso the poor rooster and drag it about with a rope around its neck."

"I not do it any more," promised Trouble. "But I want a lasso like Teddy."

"No, you're not big enough for that," his mother said. "You must wait until you are a little older. Don't bother the chickens any more."

"No, I only get de eggs," promised Baby William.

"And please don't lasso them, or you'll break them," put in Aunt Millie; but Janet thought her "eyes laughed," as she later told Teddy.

"No more lasso?" asked Trouble, looking at the rope his aunt had taken from the rooster's long neck.

"No more lasso!" exclaimed Mrs. Barton, trying not to smile, for the sight of the rooster, caught the way he had been, made even the older folks want to laugh. Ted and Janet did laugh, but they did not let Trouble see them. If he had he might have thought he had done something smart or cute, and he would try it over again the first chance he had. So they had to pretend to be sharp with him. The rooster was not hurt by being lassoed.

Afterward Trouble told how he did it. With the slip-noose of the rope in one hand and holding the rope's end in the other, Baby William walked quietly up behind the rooster and tossed the loop over its head. Then he pulled it tight and started to run, as he had seen the cow ponies galloping to pull down a horse or steer that needed to be branded or marked with the sign of the Ring Rosy Ranch. The rooster was very tame, often eating out of Aunt Millie's hand, so he was not afraid to let Trouble come up quite close to him.

One day, about a week after the Curlytops had found Clipclap in the cave, Jim Mason said he thought the pony was well enough to be ridden. Clipclap was brought out in the yard and Teddy and Janet went up to him.

The pony put his nose close to them and rubbed his head against their outstretched hands.

"See, he knows us!" cried Janet.

"And I guess he's thanking us for bringing him water," added her brother.

"And getting the doctor to cure him of poison," went on the little girl. "I'm glad he likes you, Teddy."

"And your pony likes you, too, Janet," said the little boy.

Janet's pony, Star Face, certainly seemed to like her. For he came when she called him and took lumps of sugar from her hand. He liked Teddy, too. In fact both ponies were very pretty and friendly and it would be hard to say which was the better. Janet liked hers and Teddy liked his, and that is the best thing I can say about them.

No one came to claim Clipclap. Though Uncle Frank spoke to a number of other ranchmen about finding the sick pony, none of them had ever seen Clipclap before as far as they knew. If he belonged to some other ranch it must have been far away.

"So you may feel that it is all right for you to keep your pony, Curlytop," said Uncle Frank to Teddy. "If anyone should, later, say it belongs to him, and can prove it, we'll give it up, of course."

"But I don't want to give Clipclap up!" Teddy cried.

"Well, maybe you won't have to," said his father. "But you must not keep what is not yours. Anyhow, if you should have to give up Clipclap Uncle Frank will give you another pony."

"There couldn't be any as nice as Clipclap—not even Janet's Star Face," declared Teddy.

He felt bad at the thought of having to give up his pet, but there was no need to, for as the weeks went on no one came to claim Clipclap, and Teddy counted him as his own.

By this time Teddy and Janet had learned to ride quite well for such little children. They knew how to sit in a saddle, up straight like an arrow, and not slouched down or all humped up "like a bag of meal," as Uncle Frank was wont to say. They knew how to guide their ponies by pulling on the reins to left or to right, according to which way they wanted to go.

Of course they could not ride very fast yet, and Mother Martin was just as glad they could not, for she was afraid, if they did, they might fall off and get hurt. But Teddy and Janet were careful, and they knew how to sit in the saddle with their feet in the stirrups.

"They're getting to be good little riders," said Jim Mason to Uncle Frank one day.

"I'll take 'em with me the next time I go for a short ride."

"Maybe we could find the bad Indians that took your horses, Uncle Frank," said Teddy.

"Well, I wish you could," said the owner of Ring Rosy Ranch.

The cowboys had not been able to get back the stolen horses nor find the Indians who had run them off. Other ranches, too, had been robbed and a number of head of horses and cattle had been driven away.

"We've looked all over for those Indians," said Uncle Frank, "but we can't find 'em. If you Curlytops can, I'll give you each another pony."

"I'd like Clipclap best though," announced Teddy.

"What could we do with two?" asked Janet.

"Oh, every cowboy or cowgirl, for that matter, has more than one horse when he can," said Jim Mason. "Then if one gets lame he has another to ride. But don't you Curlytops go off by yourselves looking for those bad Indians!" he warned them.

"We won't," promised Teddy. "Well only go with you or Uncle Frank."

"We don't find them," said the ranch owner. "I guess the Indians sold the horses and cattle and then they hid themselves. Well, I hope they don't take any more of my animals."

But there was more trouble ahead for Uncle Frank.

The Curlytops had a fine time on his ranch, though. When Teddy and Janet were not riding, they were watching the cowboys at work or play, for the men who looked after Uncle Frank's cattle had good times as well as hard work.

They would often come riding and swooping in from the distant fields after their day's work, yelling and shouting as well as firing off their big revolvers. But neither the Curlytops nor their mother were as frightened at this play of the cowboys as they had been at first.

"I wish I had a gun that would go bang," said Teddy one day.

"Oh, The-o-dore Mar-tin!" cried his sister, after the fashion of her mother. "If you had I'd never go riding ponyback with you—never again! I'd be afraid of you! So there!"

"Well, so would the Indians!" said Ted. However he knew he was too small to have a firearm, so he did not tease for it.

Sometimes, when Uncle Frank or his foreman, Jim Mason, went on short rides around the ranch, Teddy and Janet went with them on their ponies. Star Pace and Clipclap were two sturdy little animals, and were gentle with the children.

"Come on! Let's have a race!" Ted would call.

"All right. But don't go too fast," Janet would answer, and they would trot off, the ponies going as fast as was safe for the children.

Teddy generally won these races, for Janet, who was very tender-hearted, did not like to make her pony go as fast as it could go. Often, perhaps, if Janet had urged Star Face on she would have beaten her brother, for Clipclap still felt a little weak, now and then, from his illness.

One day a cowboy came in, riding hard from a far-off part of the ranch.

"I guess something is the matter, Jan," said Teddy, as they saw the horseman gallop past.

"What?" she asked as they noticed him talking to the foreman.

"Maybe he's found the Indians that took Uncle Frank's horses," her brother answered.

The children drew near enough to hear what the cowboy and the foreman were talking about.

"More horses gone!" exclaimed Jim Mason. "Well, we'll surely have to get after those Indians; that's all there is about it!"

"More horses stolen?" asked Daddy Martin, coming out just then.

"Yes," answered Jim Mason. "A lot of good ones. I guess more Indians must have run away from the reservation. We'll have to hunt them down!"

"Oh, I wish I could go!" sighed Teddy. "I'd like to be an Indian fighter."

"You'll have to grow a lot bigger," said his uncle, with a laugh.

Uncle Frank and some of the cowboys rode over the prairie, trying to find the stealing Indians, but they could not. Nor could they find the missing horses, either.

"It's a good thing Uncle Frank has lots of cattle," said Teddy that night when the cowboys came back to the ranch house, not having found the horse thieves. "If he didn't have he'd be poor when the Indians take his animals."

"He'll be poor if the Indians keep on the way they have been doing," said Aunt Millie. "I hope he can catch the bad men!"

Ted and Janet hoped so too, but they did not see how they could help, though Teddy wanted to. However he was kept near the house.

"Come on and see the bucking bronco, Curlytops!" called Uncle Frank to Teddy and Janet one day.

"What is it?" asked the little girl.

"A bucking bronco jumps up in the air with all four feet off the ground at once, and comes down as stiff as a board," explained Uncle Frank. "That isn't nice for the man that's in the saddle, though the cowboys know how to ride most bucking broncos, that are really sort of wild horses."

"I'd like to see 'em!" cried Teddy.

"You may," promised his uncle. "The cowboys have a bucking bronco out in the corral and they're taking turns trying to ride him. Come along if you want to see the fun."

It was fun, but some hard work, too, for one after another the cowboys fell out of the saddle of the bucking bronco as they tried to ride him.

Now and then one would stay on the wild animal's back longer than had any of his friends, not falling when the bronco leaped up in the air and came down with his legs as stiff as those of an old fashioned piano.

"Ki-yi! Yippi-i-yip!" yelled the cowboys, as they dashed about on the bucking bronco, swinging their hats or their quirts, which are short-handled whips, in the air over their heads.

They did not mind being thrown, and each one tried to ride the wild bronco. None could stay in the saddle more than a few minutes at a time though.

"Well, I guess I'll have to ride that animal myself," said Jim Mason, when all the other cowboys had tried and had fallen or jumped from the saddle. The foreman was a fine rider. "Yes, I guess I can ride that bronco," he said.

"Give the pony a chance to get his breath," suggested one of the cowboys. "I don't reckon you can ride him though, Jim."

"I'll try," was the answer.

The bronco was led to a corner of the corral, or stable yard, and tied. Then the foreman made ready to try to stay in the saddle longer than had any of his men, for when a bronco bucks it is like trying to hold on to a swing that is turning topsy-turvy.

Suddenly, as Teddy and Janet were looking at some of the funny tricks the cowboys were playing on one another, Uncle Frank gave a cry.

"Look at Trouble!" he exclaimed.

Baby William had crawled through the fence and was close to the dangerous heels of the bucking bronco.

CHAPTER XIII

MISSING CATTLE

For a moment none of the cowboys made a move. They were too frightened at what might happen to Trouble. If it had been one of their own friends who had gone into the corral where the dangerous bronco was standing, they would have known what to do.

They would have called for him to "Look out!" and the cowboy would have kept away from the animal. But it was different with Trouble. To him one horse was like another. He liked them all, and he never thought any of them would kick or bite him. The bucking bronco was most dangerous of all.

"Oh, Trouble!" exclaimed Janet softly.

"I—I'll get him!" whispered Teddy. "I can crawl in there and run and get him before that bronco—"

"You stay right where you are, Curlytop!" exclaimed Jim Mason. "We don't want you both hurt, and if you go in there now you might start that crazy horse to kicking. Stay where you are. I'll get Trouble for you."

"Maybe if I called to him he'd come," said Janet. She, too, spoke in a whisper. In fact no one had made a noise since Trouble had been seen crawling under the corral fence, close to the bucking bronco.

"No, don't call, Janet," said the foreman. "You might make the bronco give a jump, and then he'd step on your little brother. That horse is a savage one, and he's so excited now, from so many of the cowboys having tried to ride him, that he might break loose and kick Trouble. We've got to keep quiet."

The cowboys seemed to know this, for none of them said a word. They kept very still and watched Trouble.

Baby William thought he was going to have a good time. He had wandered out of the house when his mother was not looking. Seeing Ted, Janet and the cowboys down by the corral, he made up his mind that was the place for him.

"Maybe I get a horse wide," he said to himself, for he was about as eager over horses as his sister or brother, and, so far, the only rides he had had were when he sat in the saddle in front with them or with his father, and went along very slowly indeed. For they dared not let the horse go fast when Trouble was with them, and Trouble wanted to go fast.

"Me go get wide myse'f," he murmured, and then, when no one was looking, he slipped under the corral fence.

He was now toddling close to the heels of the bronco.

"Nice horsie," said Trouble in his sweetest voice. "I get on your back an' have nice wide!"

Trouble always had hard work to sound the r in ride. "Wide" he always called it.

Nearer and nearer he came to the bronco. The animal, without turning its head, knew that someone was coming up behind. Many a time a cowboy had tried to fool the savage horse that way, and leap into the saddle without being seen. But Imp, as the bronco was named, knew all those tricks.

He turned back his ears, and when a horse does that it is not a good sign. Almost always it means he is going to bite or kick.

In this case Imp would have to kick, as Trouble was too far behind to be bitten. And Imp did not seem to care that it was a little boy who was behind, and not a big cowboy. Imp was going to do his worst.

But Jim Mason was getting ready to save Trouble. Going around to the side, where he could not be seen so well, the foreman quickly leaped over the fence. And then he ran swiftly toward Trouble, never saying a word.

The bronco heard the sound of running feet. He turned his head around to see who else was coming to bother him and then, before Imp could do anything and before Trouble could reach and put his little hands on the dangerous heels, the foreman caught up Baby William and jumped back with him, out of the way in case Imp should kick.

And kick Imp did! His heels shot out as he laid his ears farther back on his head and he gave a shrill scream, as horses can when they are angry.

"No you don't! Not this time!" cried Jim Mason, as he ran back to the fence with Trouble. "And you must never go into the corral or near horses again, Trouble! Do you hear?" and the foreman spoke to Baby William as though very angry indeed. But he had to do this, for the little fellow must learn not to go into danger.

"Don't ever go in there again!" said the foreman, as he set Trouble down on the ground in a safe place.

"No, me not go," was the answer, and Baby William's lips quivered as though he were going to cry.

"Well, that's all right, old man!" said the foreman in kind tones. For he loved children and did not even like to hurt their feelings. "I didn't mean to scare you."

But he had scared Trouble, or, rather the sudden catching up of the little fellow and the pony's scream had frightened him, and Janet's baby brother began to cry, hiding his head in her dress.

But, after all, that was the best thing to make Trouble remember that he must not go in the corral, and he had soon forgotten his tears and was laughing at the funny tricks Imp cut up as Jim Mason tried to ride him.

The foreman, after he had carried Trouble safely out of the way, went back in the corral and jumped on the bucking bronco's back. Then Imp did all he could to get the man out of the saddle.

Around and around the corral dashed the cow pony, and when he found that Jim stuck on the horse began jumping up in the air—bucking as the cowboys call it. Even that did not shake the foreman to the ground.

Then, suddenly, the horse fell down. But it was not an accident. He did it on purpose, and then he began to roll over, thinking this, surely, would get that man off his back.

It did. But when Imp tried to roll over on the foreman, to hurt him, Jim Mason just laughed and jumped out of the way. He knew Imp would probably do this and he was ready for him.

Jim watched Imp, and as soon as the bronco stopped rolling and stood up again the foreman jumped into the saddle. This was too much for Imp. He made up his mind he could not get rid of such a good rider, so the horse settled down and galloped around the corral as he ought to do.

"Hurray! Jim rides him after all!" cried some of the cowboys.

"I told you I'd stick to him" said the foreman with a laugh.

"I wish I could ride that way," said Teddy, with a little sigh when Jim came out of the corral and left Imp to have a rest.

"Well, maybe you will some day," said the foreman. "You've got a good start, and there's no better place to learn to ride ponyback than at Ring Rosy Ranch."

One warm, pleasant afternoon, when they had played about the house for some time, amusing themselves at the games they were wont to pass the time with in the East, Jan called to her brother:

"Let's go and take a ride on our ponies!"

"All right," agreed Teddy. "Where'll we go?"

"Oh, not very far. Mother told us we mustn't go very far when we're alone."

"That was before we knew how to ride," declared the little boy. "I guess we ride good enough now to take long rides."

"But not now," insisted Jan. "We'll only go for a little way, or I'm not going to play."

"All right," Teddy agreed. "We won't go very far."

So they went out to the stable where their ponies were kept, and there one of the cowboys kindly saddled Clipclap and Star Face for the little Curlytops. Uncle Frank had given orders to his men that they were to let the children have the ponies whenever it was safe to ride, and this was one of the nicest days of the summer.

"Don't let 'em run away with you!" laughed the cowboy, as he helped Jan and Ted into their saddles.

"Oh, Clipclap and Star Pace won't run away!" declared the little girl. "They're too nice."

"Yes, they are nice ponies," agreed the cowboy. "Well, good-bye and good luck."

Biding up to the house, to tell their mother they were going for a ride, but would keep within sight or calling distance, Ted and Jan were soon guiding their ponies across the prairie.

The children had soon learned to sit well in the saddles, and knew how to guide their ponies. And the little animals were very safe.

"Somehow or other, I don't feel at all worried here when the children are out of my sight—I mean Teddy and Janet," said Mrs. Martin to her husband, when the Curlytops had ridden away.

"Yes, Uncle Frank's ranch does seem a safe place for them," Mr. Martin answered. "Lots of 'down East' people think the West is a dangerous place. Well, maybe it is in spots, but it is very nice here."

On over the prairies rode Teddy and Janet. Now and then the little girl would stop her pony and look back.

"What are you looking for?" Teddy asked. "Do you think Trouble is following us?"

"No, but we mustn't go too far from the house. We must stay in sight of it, mother said."

"Well, we will," promised Ted.

But, after a while, perhaps it was because it was so nice to ride along on the ponies' backs, or because the little animals went faster than Ted or Janet imagined—I don't know just how it did happen, but, all at once, Jan looked back and gave a cry.

"Why, what's the matter, Jan?" asked Teddy.

"We—we're lost!" gasped the little girl. "I can't see Uncle Frank's house anywhere!"

It was true enough. None of the ranch buildings were in sight, and for a moment Ted, too, was frightened. Then as his pony moved on, a little ahead of Jan's, the boy gave a cry of delight.

"There it is! I can see the house!" he said. "We're not lost. We were just down in a hollow I guess."

And so it was. The prairies, though they look level, are made up of little hills and valleys, or hollows. Down in between two hills one might be very near a house and yet not see it.

"Now we're all right," went on Teddy.

"Yes," agreed Janet "We're not lost anymore."

So they rode on a little farther, the ponies now and then stopping to crop a bit of the sweet grass, when, all of a sudden, Teddy, who was still a little ahead of his sister, called:

"Look there, Jan!"

"Where?"

Teddy pointed. His sister saw several men on horseback—at least that is what they looked like—coming toward them. Something about the figures seemed a bit strange to the children. Ted and Jan looked at one another and then back toward the ranch houses, which, they made sure, were not out of sight this time.

"Are they cowboys?" asked Jan of her brother.

"They—they don't just look like 'em," he said. "I mean like Uncle Frank's cowboys."

"That's what I thought," Janet added. "They look like they had blankets on—some of 'em."

She and Teddy sat on their ponies' backs and kept looking at the other figures. They were coming nearer, that was sure, and as they came closer it was more and more certain to the Curlytops that some of the strangers on the horses were wrapped in blankets.

"Oh, I know what they are!" suddenly cried Janet.

"What?"

"In—Indians!" faltered Janet. "Oh, Teddy, if they should be wild Indians!"

"Pooh!" exclaimed Teddy, trying to speak bravely. "Uncle Frank said there weren't any very wild Indians near his ranch."

"Maybe these ones wasn't near the ranch before, but they're coming near now," said Janet, so excited the words tumbled out all mixed-up like. "I'm going home!"

"I—I guess I'll go with you," added Teddy, as he turned his pony's head about. "We'd better tell Uncle Frank the Indians are coming. Maybe they want more of his horses."

"Oh, he won't let 'em have any!" cried Janet. "But they are Indians sure enough!" she went on, as she took a look over her shoulder.

And there was no doubt about it. As the group of riders came closer to the children, whose ponies did not go as fast as the larger horses, it was seen that they were indeed Indians, many of them wrapped in blankets. There were men, women, boys and girls, and some of the smaller children were carried wrapped tightly to their mothers' backs.

Tip to the ranch rode Teddy and Jan as fast as their ponies would take them without tossing off the Curlytops.

"Oh, Uncle Frank!" cried Teddy. "They 're coming!"

"A lot of 'em!" shouted Janet.

"What's that?" asked the ranchman. "Who are coming?"

"Indians to take more of your ponies!" Teddy gasped.

For a time there was some little excitement on the ranch, until one of the cowboys, riding out to see the Indians, came back and said they were not "wild" ones, but a band that went about selling baskets and other things they made. They did no harm, and for a time camped near the ranch, the children, even Trouble, going over to see them. But for some time the Curlytops did not forget the fright their first view of the Indians gave them.

In the days that followed Teddy and Janet had many rides on Clipclap and Star Face, their two nice ponies. Sometimes they were allowed to go a little way over the prairies by themselves. But when they went for a long ride Uncle Frank, Jim Mason, their father or some of the cowboys were with them.

"After a while maybe I'll learn how to ride so I can go off with you and help get the Indians that stole your horses. Do you think I can, Uncle Frank?" asked Teddy one day.

"Well, maybe, Curlytop. We surely must find those Indians, for I don't like to lose all those horses. As soon as I get some of my work done I'll have another look for them."

And then, a few days later, more bad news came to Uncle Frank. With his cowboys he was getting some cattle ready to ship away to a distant city, from where they were to be sent still farther away in a train of cattle cars, when a cowboy, who seemed much excited, came riding up to the corral.

He looked very tired and warm, for the weather was hot, and his horse was covered with flecks of foam, as though it had been ridden hard and far.

"What's the matter, Henry?" asked Uncle Frank.

"Indian thieves!" was the answer. "A band of the Indians have run away with a lot of your best cattle!"

"They have?" cried Uncle Frank. "How do you know?"

"I saw 'em, and I chased 'em. But they got away from me. Maybe if we start right out now we can catch 'em and get back the cattle."

"Then we'll go!" cried Uncle Frank.

Teddy and Janet were very much excited when they saw the cowboys saddling their mustangs ready for the chase.

CHAPTER XIV
LOOKING FOR INDIANS

"Can't we come along?" asked Teddy, as he saw Uncle Frank lead his horse out of the corral.

"And I want to come, too!" added Janet.

"Oh, no! We couldn't think of letting you!" answered Uncle Frank. "Come on, boys! Get ready. We'll have to ride fast!"

"We can ride fast!" added Teddy. "You said, the other day, Uncle Frank, I could ride real good!"

"So you can, Curlytop."

"Then why can't we come? Jan — she's a good rider, too!"

"Why the idea of you children thinking you can go off on a hunt for Indians!" exclaimed their mother.

"We want to go — awful much!" Teddy murmured.

"Not this time, Curly boy," said the ranchman. "We may have to be out all night, and it looks like rain. You stay at home with Janet, and I'll tell you all about it when I come back."

"Will you, truly?"

"Truly I will."

"And if you get any Indians will you bring 'em here?" Teddy demanded.

"No, don't!" cried Janet quickly. "I don't want to see any Indians."

"But they're tame ones," said her brother.

"They can't be awful tame, else they wouldn't run away with Uncle Frank's cows," declared the little girl.

"That's right!" laughed Uncle Frank. "I guess we won't bring any Indians here, Curlytop, even if we catch 'em, which we may not do as they have a good start of us. Anyhow we'll have to turn the Redmen back to their reservation where they belong if we get any of them. We'll just take my cattle and horses away, if we can, and tell the Indians to go home and be good."

"Will they do it?" asked Daddy Martin.

"It's hard to say," answered Uncle Frank. "I'd like to make 'em stop taking my animals, though. Well, I guess we'll start. We'll be back as soon as we can."

So he rode off with his cowboys after the Indians. The cowboy who had ridden in with the news went back with the others to show them where he had last seen the cattle thieves.

He stopped at the ranch house long enough, though, to get something to eat, and then rode away again. But he found time to talk a while to the Curlytops.

"Where did you see the Indians?" Teddy asked while the cowboy was eating and Uncle Frank and the others getting ready for the chase.

"Oh, I was giving my pony a drink at the spring in the rocks when I saw the Indians across the prairie — field, I guess you'd call it back East."

"Well, the prairies are big fields," observed Janet.

"So they are, Curly girl," laughed the cowboy. "Well, it was while I was watering my horse that I saw the Indians."

"You mean at the spring in the rocks where Jan and I found Clipclap in the cave?" Teddy asked.

"That's the place, Curlytop. I chased after them to see which way they were driving off your Uncle Frank's cattle, but I saw they were too many for me, so I came on back as fast as my horse would bring me."

"Was there a lot of Indians?" Teddy inquired.

"Quite a few," answered the cowboy. "Well, now I've got to go and help chase them," and he hurried through his meal and rode off with Uncle Frank and the others.

"Say, I wish we could go, don't you, Janet?" asked Teddy of his sister, when they were left by themselves near the corral.

"No, I don't! I don't want to chase Indians!"

"Well, I'd chase 'em and you could watch me."

"You're not big enough," said the little girl. "Indians are awful big. Don't you remember the one we saw at the station?"

"Yes. But maybe the ones that took Uncle Frank's ponies are little Indians."

"I don't care," Janet said. "I don't want to chase after any of 'em. I don't like 'em."

"All right—then I won't go," decided Teddy. "But let's go and take a ride on our ponies."

"Yes, I'll do that," agreed Janet, and soon, having had one of the cowboys who had been left behind at Ring Rosy Ranch saddle Clipclap and Star Face, the Curlytops started for their ride.

"Don't go too far!" called Mrs. Martin after the children.

"No, we won't," they promised.

"I wants to go wide too!" begged Trouble. "I 'ikes a wide on a ponyback."

"Not now, my dear," his mother said. "We'll go in the shade and pick flowers," and she carried him away where he would not see Teddy and Janet go off, for that made Trouble fretful. He wanted to be with them.

Over the prairie rode Janet and Ted. Their ponies went slowly, for the children had been told not to ride fast when they were alone. But, after a while, Ted got tired of this slow motion.

"Let's have a race, Jan!" he called. "I can beat you from here to that hill," and he pointed to one not far away.

"Mother said we couldn't ride fast," objected the little girl.

"Well, we won't ride very fast," agreed Ted. "Come on, just a little run."

Janet, too, wanted to go a bit faster, and so, when her pony was in a line with Ted's, she called sharply:

"Gid-dap, Star Face!"

"Gid-dap, Clipclap!" cried Teddy.

The two ponies started to run.

"Oh, I'm going to beat! I'm going to beat!" Janet cried, for she saw that Star Face was getting ahead of Clipclap.

"No you're not!" shouted Teddy, and he touched his heel to the pony's flank. Clipclap gave a jump forward, and then something happened.

Teddy took a flying leap, and right over Clipclap's head he sailed, coming down on his hands and knees some distance off. Clipclap fell down and rolled over in the grass while Janet kept on toward the hill that marked the end of the race.

The little girl reached this place first, not being able to stop her pony when she saw what had happened to Teddy. But as soon as she could turn around she rode back to him and asked anxiously:

"Are you hurt, Ted?"

"No — no. I — I guess not," he answered slowly.

"Is Clipclap?" asked Janet.

The pony answered for himself by getting up, giving himself a shake and then beginning to eat some grass.

"What happened?" Janet questioned further. "Why didn't you come on and race with me? I won!"

"Yes, I guess you did," admitted Teddy, getting up and brushing the dust off his clothes. "But I'd 'a' beaten you, only my pony stumbled and he threw me over his head. I went right over his head; didn't I Janet?"

"Yes, you did, Teddy. And you looked awful funny! But I'm glad you're not hurt."

"So'm I."

"What made Clipclap stumble?" asked the little girl.

"I guess he stepped in a gopher's hole," answered her brother.

"Let's look," proposed Janet.

Brother and sister went to the place where Clipclap had stumbled. There they saw a little hole in the ground. It was the front, or maybe the back, door of the home of a little animal called a gopher, which burrows under the earth. A gopher is a sort of squirrel-like rat, and on the prairies they make many holes which are dangerous if a horse suddenly steps into them. Prairie dogs are another species of animal that burrow on the Western plains, making holes into which horses or ponies often step, breaking their legs and throwing their riders.

This time nothing had happened except that Teddy and the pony had been shaken up. The pony might have broken a leg but did not, nor was Teddy even scratched.

Cowboys always dread gopher and prairie dog holes, especially at night when they can not be so easily seen.

"Oh, I know what let's do!" exclaimed Janet, when she found that her brother was all right.

"What?" asked Teddy.

"Let's wait here until the gopher comes up!"

"All right. Then we'll catch him and take him home to Trouble."

CHAPTER XV
TROUBLE "HELPS"

Janet and Teddy sat beside the gopher hole, while their ponies, not far from them, ate the sweet grass of the prairie. Clipclap and Star Face did not wander away, even if they were not tied to a hitching post. For Western horses and cow ponies are trained to stand where their master leaves them, if he will but toss the reins over their heads and let them rest on the ground.

When a pony sees that this has been done he will never run away, unless perhaps something frightens him very much. It may be that he thinks, when the reins are over his head and down on the ground, they are tied to something, so he could not run away if he wanted to.

At any rate, Clipclap and Star Face stayed where Ted and Janet left them, and the little Curlytops watched the gopher hole.

"I wonder when he'll come out," said Janet after a bit.

"Shs-s-s-s!" whispered Teddy. "Don't talk!"

"Why not?" asked his sister.

"'Cause you might scare him. You mustn't talk any more than if you were fishing."

"A gopher isn't a fish!"

"I know it," said Teddy. "But you've got to keep quiet."

So he and Janet remained very quiet, watching the hole. Suddenly Janet gave Teddy a slight tap with her hand. He had looked off to see if the ponies were all right.

"What's the matter?" asked Teddy.

"Hush!" whispered Janet. "There he is."

She pointed to the gopher's hole. Teddy saw a tiny black nose and a pair of sparkling eyes as a head was thrust a little way out of the burrow.

"I'll get him!" cried the little boy.

With outstretched hand he made a grab toward the hole. But his fingers only grasped a lot of dirt and stones. The gopher had dived down back into his hole as soon as he saw Teddy's first move.

"Oh, he got away!" said Janet sorrowfully.

"Ill get him next time," declared Teddy.

But he did not. Three or four times more the little animal put his small head and bright eyes out of the top of the hole, and each time Teddy made a grab for him; but the gopher was too quick. Finally Janet said:

"I guess we better go home, Teddy."

"Why?"

"Oh, it's getting late, and I'm getting hungry."

"So'm I. I'll wait until he comes up once more and then well go."

Once more the gopher peeped up, as if wondering why in the world those two strange children did not go away and let him alone. Ted made a grab for him, but missed and then the little boy said:

"Come on, Jan. Now we'll go home!"

"And we haven't any nice little gopher to take to Trouble," said Janet sadly.

"Oh, well, maybe it would bite him if we did catch one," reflected her brother. "I'll take him some of these pretty stones," and he picked up some from the ground. "He'll like to play with these."

Teddy whistled for his pony and Clipclap came slowly up to his little master. Janet held out a bunch of grass to Star Face and her pony, just as he had been taught, came up to her. Teddy helped his sister get up in the saddle. It was not hard for them, as the ponies were small, and Jim Mason had showed them how to put one foot in the stirrup, and then, with one hand on the saddle and the other grasping both the bridle and the pony's mane, give a jump that carried them up. But though Janet could mount her pony alone Teddy always helped her when he was with her by holding the stirrup.

"Let's have another race home," suggested Teddy, when they had started.

"No," answered his sister. "You might fall some more and get hurt. We'll ride slow."

So they did, though Teddy was anxious for a good, fast gallop.

"Well, did you have a nice time?" asked Mother Martin, as they came to the house after putting away their ponies.

"We had lots of fun," answered Janet "Teddy fell off his pony —"

"Fell off his pony!" cried her mother.

"He threw me!" explained Ted, and then he told what had happened.

"An' didn't you catch noffin for me?" asked Trouble, who heard his brother telling the story of his adventure.

"I brought you these nice stones," and Teddy took them out of his pocket. "You can play with them, Trouble."

Baby William laughed and sat down to play with the stones.

"Did the cowboys come back with the Indians?" asked Teddy of Aunt Millie when she was giving him and Janet some bread and jam to eat.

"No, not yet, Curlytop. I expect Uncle Frank and the boys will be gone all night."

"Will they have a house to sleep in?" asked Janet.

"No, unless they happen to be near one when it gets dark. But they took their blankets with them, and it's so warm that they'll just wrap up in them and sleep out on the prairie," said Aunt Millie.

"Won't they be hungry?" Teddy inquired, as he took a big bite of the bread and jam.

"Oh, no! Don't you remember I told you they always take something to eat with them when they go out this way? They are used to camping on the prairies, and they know how to make a fire, broil the bacon and make their coffee," answered Aunt Millie. "You need never worry about Uncle Frank and his cowboys. They'll be all right."

And so they were. It was not until the next afternoon that the party which had gone out to chase the Indians came back. They were tired, because they had ridden a good many miles, but they said they had slept well and had had enough to eat.

"Did you catch the Indians?" asked Teddy eagerly.

"No, Curlytop," answered Uncle Frank. "I'm sorry to say we did not. They got away from us."

"Did you see them?" asked Daddy Martin.

"Yes, but they were a long way off. Too far for us to get at them."

"And did they have your cattle with them?"

"Yes, they had a lot of my best animals. I guess they must be hiding away somewhere among the hills and mountains. We came pretty close to them at one time, and they suddenly disappeared. It seems as if they must have gone into a big hole or cave. We couldn't find them."

"Are you going to look any more?" Teddy questioned. "And if you do go, Uncle Frank, please can't I go too?"

"Well, most likely we will have another hunt for the Indians," answered the ranchman, "but I'm afraid we couldn't take you along, Curlytop."

"Why not, Uncle Frank?"

"Oh, you might get hurt."

"Well, can I see the Indians after you catch 'em?"

"Oh, yes, I guess I can promise you that," and Uncle Frank smiled at Daddy Martin.

"And can I ask them to make me a bow and arrows?" went on Teddy.

"Yes, you can ask them, but I don't believe they will," Uncle Frank replied. "These Indians aren't very nice. They're quite bad, in fact, and we all wish they'd stay where they belong and not come off their reservation and steal our cattle and horses."

"Well, I'm going to ask one to make me a bow and some arrows when you catch 'em," decided Teddy.

That afternoon Teddy saw his sister trying to do something with bits of string and sticks in a shady spot on the porch.

"What are you making, Jan," he asked. "A cat's cradle?"

"Pooh! you don't make a cat's cradle with sticks," said the little girl.

"Well, I thought maybe it was a new kind, or maybe a kitten's cradle," laughed Teddy.

"Nope; it isn't that either," went on Janet, as she kept on twisting the strings around the sticks.

"Well, what are you making?"

"A bow and arrow."

"Ho! Ho!" laughed Jan's brother "You can't make a bow and arrow that way. Anyhow you don't need a string for an arrow."

"I know that!" Jan said. "But I'm making the bow first, and then I'm going to make the arrow. The arrow part is what you shoot, isn't it, Ted?"

"Yes," he answered. "I'll help you, Jan. I didn't mean to laugh at you," he went on, for he saw that Janet was very much in earnest about what she was doing. "I know how to make a bow and arrows."

"Oh, please show me!" begged Janet. "I want to know how to shoot like the Indians."

Teddy, however, did not have much better luck making the bow than his sister had had. The trouble was that the sticks Janet had picked up were not the right kind. They would not bend, and to make a bow that shoots arrows a piece of wood that springs, or bends, is needed. For it is the springy action of the wood that shoots the arrow on its way.

After trying two or three times, each time finding something wrong, Teddy said:

"Oh, I don't guess I can make a bow, either. Let's play something else."

"What'll we play?" asked Janet.

Teddy thought for a few moments. Playing out at Uncle Frank's ranch was different from playing at home. In some ways it was not so easy, for at home if the Curly-tops could not think up any way to have fun by themselves, they could run down the street and find some other boys and girls. But here there were no streets, and no other boys or girls unless Teddy and Janet went a long way to look for them, and they could not do that.

"I know what we can do," said Teddy, after a while. "We can get some blankets and cookies and play cowboy."

"How can you play cowboy with cookies and blankets?"

"I'll show you," Teddy answered, as he went into the house to get the things he wanted. He soon came out with some old quilts and the cookies, which were in a paper bag.

"Now," went on Janet's brother, "we'll go off on the prairie and make believe it's night and we have to stay out like the cowboys when they went after Uncle Frank's horses."

"Oh, that'll be fun!" cried Janet, and then she and Ted rolled themselves up in the old quilts and pretended to go to sleep on the soft grass of the prairie, making believe it was night, though of course it was not, for the sun was shining. Then they ate the cookies, pretending they were bacon, sandwiches, cake and other things that cowboys like.

Two or three days later Uncle Frank and the cowboys went out again to look for the Indians, but they did not find them. From other ranches word came of cattle and horses that had been stolen; and more cowboys were hired to keep watch over the animals that had to be left out in the big fields to eat their fill of grass. No barn was large enough to hold them.

Meanwhile Teddy and Janet were learning how to ride better each day. They could go quite fast now, though they were not allowed to make their ponies gallop except on ground where Uncle Frank knew there were no holes in which the animals might stumble.

Sometimes Daddy and Mother Martin went to ride with the children, and then they had good times together, taking their lunch and staying all day out on the prairie or in a shady grove of trees.

One day Ted and Janet saw some cowboys driving a number of ponies to the corral near the ranch buildings. Some of the animals were quite wild and went racing about as though they would like to run far off and not come back.

But the cowboys knew how to take care of the ponies. They rode around them, keeping them together in a bunch, and if one started to get away the cowboys would fire their revolvers and yell, so the pony would become frightened and turn back.

"Did you take these ponies away from the Indians?" asked Teddy, as he saw the little animals turned into the corral and the gate shut on them.

"No, these are some that have been running wild in a field away over at the far end of my ranch," explained Uncle Frank. "I had them brought in, as I'm going to ship some away to be sold."

"Come on, we'll go and look at the ponies," called Ted to his sister. "Are they very wild?" he asked Jim Mason, who had helped the cowboys bring them to the ranch corral.

"Yes, some of 'em are pretty wild," was the answer. "We had hard work making them come along. They want to get loose and do as they please."

Ted and Janet climbed up on the corral fence to look at the ponies. A few were somewhat tame, and allowed the Curlytops to pat them. But others were very wild, and ran about as though looking for a place to jump the fence or get out through a hole. But the fence was good and strong. It was high and had no holes in it.

"Lots of ponies!" murmured Trouble, as he toddled after his brother and sister to the corral.

"Yes, lots of 'em," agreed Janet. "You'll soon be a big boy and you can have a pony to ride like brother and sister."

"Trouble want pony now!" he exclaimed.

"Oh, no, not now," Janet said as she helped him get up on the lowest board of the fence, part of which was wooden, so he could look in better.

"What they run around like that for?" asked Trouble, as he saw some of the ponies racing about the corral.

"They want to get out," Janet answered.

"Trouble go help," murmured the little fellow, but Janet either did not hear what he said or she paid no attention, for just then two of the ponies had a race together around the corral and she and Ted wanted to see which would win.

Trouble got down off the fence and went around to the gate. His brother and sister did not notice him until, all at once, Janet, missing her little brother, cried:

"Where's Trouble?"

"I don't know," Ted answered. "Maybe he—Oh, look, Janet!" he suddenly cried. "The corral gate is open and all the ponies are running out!"

"Oh, that's right! They are!" Janet then screamed. "But where is Trouble?"

"I don't know. I guess he—Oh, there he is!" and Teddy pointed to a spot near the gate.

There stood Trouble between the fence and the big gate which had swung back on its hinges.

"Oh, look at 'em run!" cried Janet.

"They're all running out!" added Teddy excitedly. "I wonder who let 'em loose."

"Maybe it was Trouble," suggested Janet. "Oh, it was!" she went on. "Trouble must have opened the gate and let the ponies loose!"

CHAPTER XVI
ON THE TRAIL

Trouble had done that very thing. The little fellow had not meant to do any harm, and certainly thought he was doing something to help, but really he made a great deal of work for Uncle Frank and the cowboys.

The corral, or yard where the half-tamed horses were kept while they were being got ready to send away, was closed by a large gate, but one easy to open if you knew how. All one had to do was to pull on a little handle, which snapped a spring and the gate would swing open.

Horses and cattle could not open the gate, for they could not reach the handle, even if any of them had known enough to do anything like that.

But Trouble had watched Uncle Frank or some of the cowboys open the gate by pulling on the handle; and now he did it himself. Then, of course, when the ponies saw the open gate they raced out.

"Get after 'em!" cried Uncle Frank who came galloping up on his horse to find out what was the matter. "Get after the ponies, boys! Round them up!"

"Round up," is what cowboys call riding around a lot of horses or cattle to keep the animals in one place or to drive them where they should go. Uncle Frank wanted his cowboys to ride after the runaway ponies and drive them back into the corral.

As the wild little horses trotted out through the gate, behind which Trouble stood, well out of danger, the cowboys rode after them, yelling and shouting and shooting their revolvers.

"What a lot of noise!" cried Janet, covering her ears with her hands as she got down off the fence.

"I like it!" laughed Teddy. "It's like a Wild West show!"

Indeed it was, in a way, but it meant a lot of work for Uncle Frank and his men. For all the ponies ran out of the corral and were scattering over the prairie.

"Oh, Trouble! did you let the horses out?" asked Janet, as her little brother came out from behind the gate and toddled toward her and Ted. The runaway horses were now well out of the way. "Did you open the gate?"

"Yes. I did open gate," Trouble answered, smiling.

"What for?" asked Teddy.

"Help little horses get out," said Trouble. "Them want to get out and Trouble help them. Trouble 'ike ponies!"

"Oh, but, my dear, you shouldn't have done it!" chided Mother Martin, who had come out of the house to find out what all the excitement was about. "That was very naughty of you. See all the work you have made for Uncle Frank and his men."

"Horses run out when Trouble open gate," was the only reply Baby William made.

"Yes, I know," went on his mother. "But it was wrong! You must never again open any gates on Uncle Frank's ranch. Just think — the horses might have stepped on you or kicked you!"

"We didn't see him near the gate or we'd have stopped him," put in Teddy.

"That's true," added Janet. "The first we saw was the ponies going out, and then we saw Trouble behind the gate."

"He didn't mean to be bad," said his mother, as she carried him back to the house, "but he has made a lot of work. I'll have to punish him by not letting him out to play for an hour or so. Then he'll remember not to open gates again, whether he thinks he is helping horses or not."

And, though Trouble cried very hard, he was kept in the house. For, as his mother had said, he must have something to make him remember not to do such a thing again.

Meanwhile Uncle Frank and the cowboys were busy rounding up the runaway ponies. The little horses, tired of being cooped up in the corral, raced about, kicking up their heels and glad to be out on the prairie again. But the cowboys knew how to handle them.

Around and around the drove of half-wild ponies rode the yelling and shouting men, firing off many blank cartridges to scare the little animals back into the corral.

Some of the ponies, frightened by the noise, did turn back. They ran up to the corral gate, which was still open, and sniffed at the fence. They may have said to themselves:

"We don't like it, being shut up in there, but maybe well have to go back in, for we don't like being shouted at, and we don't like the bang-bang noises like thunder."

But, even when some of the ponies had run back as far as the corral gate they did not go in. Once again they turned around and would have galloped across the prairie again. But Uncle Frank shouted:

"Get after them, boys! Drive those few in and the rest will follow after like sheep! Get after them!"

So the cowboys rode up on their own swift ponies, that seemed to be having a good time, and then the other ponies nearest the corral gate were turned in through it. Then as the rest were driven up they did as the first ones had done and galloped back where they had been before Trouble let them out.

One after another the ponies ran back into the corral until every one was there. Then Uncle Frank closed the gate, and this time he locked it so that no one could open it without the key. But no one would try, not even Trouble, for, crying and sobbing to be allowed to go out and play, he had been given a lesson that he would not soon forget.

"I'm sorry I had to punish him," said Mother Martin to the Curlytops, when they came in after the ponies were once more in the corral, "but I just had to. Work on a ranch is hard enough without little boys letting the horses run wild after they have once been caught."

"Oh, well, no great harm was done," said Uncle Frank with a good-natured laugh, "though it did make us ride pretty hard for a while. Come on, Trouble, I'll take you ponyback!"

This was what Trouble liked, and he soon dried his tears and sat on the saddle in front of Uncle Frank as happy as could be. Janet and Ted got out their ponies, and rode with Uncle Frank and Trouble around the outside of the corral, looking at the little horses inside the fence. They were quieter now, and were eating some oats the cowboys had put out for them.

Two or three days after this, when the ponies had been driven away to the railroad station to be shipped to a far-off state, a cowboy came riding in with news that he had seen a band of two or three Indians pass along the prairie near the rocks where Teddy and Janet had found Clipclap.

"If we ride after them," said the cowboy, "maybe we can find where the other Indians are, and where they have hidden your horses and cattle, Mr. Barton."

"That's it!" exclaimed Uncle Frank. "We'll get on the trail after these Indians. I'm sure they must have some of my animals hidden away in the hills, for I would have heard of it if they had sold them around here. We'll get on the trail!"

"What's the trail, Daddy?" asked Teddy of his father.

"Oh, it means the marks the Indians' ponies may have left in the soft ground," said Mr. Martin. "Uncle Frank and his cowboys will try to trail, or follow, the marks of the horses' feet, and see where the Indians have gone."

"Can't I come?" asked Teddy. "I can ride good now!"

"Oh, no indeed you can't go!" cried Mother Martin. "Are you going?" she asked her husband.

"Yes," he answered. "I think I'll go on the trail with Uncle Frank."

CHAPTER XVII

THE CURLYTOPS ALONE

Teddy and Janet sat on a bench outside the cowboys' bunkhouse, as their father, Uncle Frank and a number of the ranchmen rode away over the prairies on the trail of the Indians. The Curlytops did not seem very happy.

"Don't you wish we could go, Jan?" asked Teddy, after he and his sister had sat in silence for some time.

"I just guess I do!" she exclaimed. "I can ride good, too. Almost as good as you, Ted, and I don't see why we couldn't go!"

"Yes, you ride nice, Jan," said her brother. "But I thought you were afraid of Indians."

"I used to be, but I'm not any more. Anyway, if you'd stay with me I wouldn't be. And, anyhow, Uncle Frank says the Indians won't hurt us."

"Course they won't! I'm not afraid! I'd go on the trail after 'em if they'd let us."

"So would I. We could throw stones at 'em if they tried to hurt us, Teddy."

"Yes. Or we could ride our ponies fast and get away. Uncle Frank told me the Indians didn't have any good ponies, and that's why they took his."

"But we can't go," said Janet with a sigh.

"No; we've got to stay at home."

A little later a cowboy came limping out of the bunkhouse. His name was Sim Body, but all his friends called him "Baldy" because he had so little hair on his head.

"Hello, Curlytops!" cried Baldy in a jolly voice, for he was always good-natured. Even now he was jolly, though he had a lame foot where a horse had stepped on it. That is why he was not on the trail after the Indians with the other cowboys.

"Hello," answered Teddy, but he did not speak in a jolly voice.

"Why, what's the matter?" asked Baldy with a laugh, as he limped to the bench and sat down near the two children. "You act as sad and gloomy as if there wasn't a Christmas or a New Year's any more, to say nothing of Fourth of July and birthdays! What's the matter? Seems to me, if I had all the nice, curly hair you two have, I'd be as happy as a horned toad and I'd go around singing all day long," and Baldy rubbed his hand over his own smooth head and laughed.

"I don't like my hair," grumbled Teddy. "It's always getting snarled and the comb gets stuck in it."

"And it does in mine, too," added Janet. "And mother pulls when she tries to untangle it. Mine's longer than Ted's."

"Yes, and nicer, for that reason," went on Baldy. "Though I'd be glad if I had even half of yours, Teddy. But never mind about that. I won't take your hair, though I'd like to know what makes you both so gloomy-like. Can't you smile?"

Ted and Janet could not help laughing at Baldy, he seemed so funny. He was a good friend of theirs.

"We can't go on the trail after Indians," said Janet. "We want to go, but we've got to stay here."

"And we can ride our ponies good, too," went on Teddy. "Uncle Frank said we could."

"Yes, you're getting to be pretty good riders," admitted Baldy. "But that isn't saying you're big enough to go on a trail after Indians. Of course these Indians may not be very bad, and maybe they aren't the ones that took our horses. But riding on a trail takes a long while, and maybe the boys will be out all night in the open. You wouldn't like that."

"We went camping with our grandpa once," declared Teddy.

"And we slept in a tent," added his sister.

"And we saw a funny blue light and we thought it was a ghost but it wasn't," continued Teddy.

"Hum! A ghost, eh?" laughed Baldy. "Well, I've never been on a trail after one of them, but I've trailed Indians—and helped catch 'em, too."

"How do you do it?" asked Teddy eagerly.

"Well, you just keep on riding—following the trail you know—until you catch up to those you're after. Sometimes you can't see any marks on the ground and you have to guess at it."

"And do the Indians ride on ahead and try to get away?" asked Janet.

"Indeed they do. When they know we're after 'em they ride as fast as they can. That is, if they've done wrong, like taking horses or cattle that aren't theirs. We just keep chasing 'em until we get close enough to arrest 'em."

"It's like a game of tag, isn't it?" asked Janet.

"Well, yes, you could call it sort of like that," admitted Baldy, with another laugh. "But it's a kind of game of tag that little boys and girls can't very well play."

"Not even when they have ponies?" asked Teddy.

"Well, of course, having a pony makes it easier to keep on the trail. You couldn't go very far walking over the prairies—at least none of us do. We all ride. But I'll tell you some stories about cowboys and Indians and that will amuse you for a while. Like to hear 'em?"

"Oh, yes!" cried Teddy.

"Very much, thank you," added Janet, a little more politely but still just as eagerly as her brother.

So Baldy, sitting on the bench in front of the bunkhouse and resting his lame foot on a saddle on the ground, told the Curlytops stories of his cowboy life—of sleeping out on the prairies keeping watch over the cattle, of Indians or other bad men who would come and try to steal them, and how he and his friends had to give chase to get the steers or ponies back.

"Did you ever get captured by the Indians?" asked Teddy.

"Well, yes, once I was," answered the cowboy.

"Oh, tell us about it!" begged the little Curlytop chap. "I love to hear stories about Indians! Don't you, Jan?"

"I like stories—yes," said the little girl. "But if you're going to tell a story about Indians, Mr. Baldy, maybe it'll be a scary one, and I don't like scary stories."

"I do!" exclaimed Ted. "The scarier they are the better I like 'em!"

Baldy laughed as he said:

"Well, I guess, seeing as how the little lady doesn't like scary stories, I'd better tell one that isn't. We must please the ladies, you know, Teddy."

"Oh, yes, I know that," the little boy said. "But after you tell the not-scary story, Mr. Baldy, couldn't you tell me one that is scary—a real, terrible scary one. You can take me out behind the barn where Jan can't hear it."

"Well, maybe I could do that," agreed the good-natured cowboy, laughing at the Curlytops. "Now then for the not-scary story."

"And you don't have to take Teddy out behind the barn to tell him the scary one," put in Janet. "You could stay here, and I could cover up my ears with my hands when you came to the terrible parts, couldn't I? Is there any parts in it that isn't scary? I'd like to hear them, Mr. Baldy."

"Well, I guess we can fix it that way," said the cowboy. "Now the first story I'm going to tell you, is how I was captured by the Indians," and the children sat closer to him and waited eagerly.

"Once upon a time," said Baldy, "a lot of Indians lived not far from the house where I lived."

"Weren't you afraid?" asked Janet.

"Please don't ask questions till he tells the story," begged Teddy.

"All right," agreed his sister, and Baldy went on:

"No, I wasn't much afraid, or if I was I've forgotten it now, as it was quite a while ago. Anyhow, one day I was out on the prairie, picking flowers, I think, for I know I used to like flowers, and, all of a sudden, along came a lot of Indians on horses, and one of them picked me up and took me right away with him, on the horse in front of him.

"The horse was a strong one, and could easily carry both of us, and though I wiggled around a good bit and yelled, the Indian didn't let go of me. On and on he rode, carrying me off, and the other Indians rode ahead of us, and on either side. I couldn't get away, no matter how I tried.

"After a while the Indians, who had been out hunting, came to where their tents were. This was their camp, and then I was lifted down off the horse and given to a squaw."

Teddy simply had to ask some questions now.

"A squaw is a Indian lady, isn't she?"

"Yes," answered Baldy, "that's what she is."

"Well, I shouldn't think she'd want to take you," went on the little boy. "I thought the Indian men always kept the prisoners, and you were a prisoner, weren't you?"

"Yes," answered Baldy, and there was a queer smile on his face, "but I guess I forgot to tell you that the time I was captured by the Indians I was a little boy, not as big as you, Curlytop. And the reason they picked me up off the prairie was that I had wandered away from my home and was lost. So the nice squaw kept me until one of the Indian men had time to take me home."

"Then didn't the Indians hurt you?" asked Janet.

"Not a bit. They were very good to me," the cowboy said. "Some of them knew my father and mother. That's the only time I was ever captured by the Indians, and I'm afraid it wasn't very much of a story."

"Oh, it was very nice," said Teddy politely.

"And not a bit scary, except a little teeny bit at first," added Janet. "Can you tell us another, Mr. Baldy?"

"Well, I guess I can," said the good-natured cowboy. So he told other tales of what had happened to him on the prairies, for he had lived in the West all his life, and knew much about it.

Teddy and Janet were very glad to hear these stories, but listening to them made Ted, at least, wish all the more that he could have gone with his father and his Uncle Frank on the trail after the Indians.

Then Baldy was called away by another cowboy, who wanted to ask him something about a sick horse, and Teddy and Janet were called by their mother to take care of Trouble for a while.

It was still morning, the cowboys having ridden away before dinner. They had taken with them enough to eat, even if they had to stay out all night.

"I wants a wide!" announced Trouble, when his brother and sister came in to get him.

"Could we give him a little ride on our ponies?" asked Teddy of his mother.

"Yes, I think so. But don't go far away from the stable. Are any of the cowboys out there to help you saddle?"

Saddling, which meant buckling the leather seat tightly around the pony, was something Teddy and Janet could not yet do very well for themselves. It takes strong fingers to tighten the straps.

"Yes, Baldy is out there," Janet said.

"How often have I told you not to call the men by their nicknames?" asked Mother Martin with a smile. "It isn't nice for children to do that."

"But, please, Mother, we don't know his other name very well," said Teddy. "Everybody calls him Baldy."

"Yes, that's right," agreed Aunt Millie. "I do myself. I guess he doesn't mind."

"Very well, if he'll saddle your ponies for you, take Trouble for a little ride," agreed Mrs. Martin. "But be careful."

The Curlytops said they would, and they were soon taking turns riding Trouble on the saddles in front of them. Clipclap and Star Face liked the children and were well-behaved ponies, so there was no danger in putting Trouble on the back of either as long as Ted or Janet held him.

"But don't go riding off with him on the trail after the Indians," said Baldy, playfully shaking his finger at the Curlytops.

"We won't!" they promised.

Up and down on the paths among the ranch buildings rode the children. Trouble was allowed to hold the ends of the reins, and he thought he was guiding the ponies, but really Teddy and Janet did that.

But finally even such fun as riding ponyback tired Trouble. He wanted something else to do, and said:

"Le's go an' s'ide downhill on hay in de barn."

Teddy and Janet knew what that meant. They had learned this kind of fun at Grandpa Martin's Cherry Farm. Here, on Ring Rosy Ranch, there was a large barn filled with hay, and there was plenty of room to slide down in the mow, or place where the hay was put away.

"Come on!" cried Janet. "Well give him a good slide, Teddy."

A little later the Curlytops and Baby William were laughing and shouting in the barn, rolling down and tumbling over one another, but not getting hurt, for the hay was too soft.

Pretty soon the dinner horn blew and, with good appetites from their morning's fun, the children hurried in to get something to eat.

"This is a good dinner!" announced Teddy as he passed his plate a second time.

"Yes," agreed Mother Martin. "I hope your father and the cowboys have as good."

"Oh, they'll have plenty—never fear!" laughed Uncle Frank's wife. "They never go hungry when they're on the trail."

After dinner Trouble went to sleep, as he generally did, and Teddy and Janet were left to themselves to find amusement.

"Let's go for another ride," suggested Teddy.

"All right," agreed Janet.

The saddles had not been taken off their ponies. Their mother and Aunt Millie saw them go out and, supposing they were only going to ride around the barn and ranch buildings, as they had done before, said nothing to them.

But Ted was no sooner in the saddle than he turned to his sister and said:

"Jan, why can't we go riding the trail after the Indians?"

"What! We two alone?"

"Yes. We know the way over to the rocks where we found Clipclap in the cave, and from there we can ride farther on, just like daddy and Uncle Frank. Come on!"

Janet thought for a minute. She wanted to go as much as did Teddy. It did not seem very wrong.

"Well, we'll ride a little way," she said. "But we've got to come back before dark."

"All right," agreed Teddy. "We will!"

And the Curlytops rode away over the prairie.

CHAPTER XVIII
LOST

Clipclap and Star Face, the two sturdy little ponies, trotted bravely along, carrying Teddy and Janet on their backs. The ponies did not wonder where they were going—they hardly ever did that. They were satisfied to go wherever their master or mistress guided them, for they knew the children would be good to them.

"Do you s'pose we'll find any Indians?" asked Janet after a while.

"Maybe," answered Teddy. "Are you scared?"

"No," replied his sister slowly. "I was just thinking maybe we could find 'em, and get back Uncle Frank's horses, even if the cowboys didn't."

"Maybe we could!" cried Teddy. "That would be great! Wouldn't daddy be surprised!"

"And Uncle Frank, too!" added Janet

"Yes, and the cowboys! Then they'd think we could ride all right!" went on Ted.

"Come on, let's hurry! Gid-dap!" he called to Clipclap.

"Where are we going first?" asked Janet.

"To the rocks, where we found my pony in the cave," answered her brother, as he patted the little animal on the neck. "The cowboy said he saw the Indians near there."

"Maybe they're hiding in the cave," suggested Janet.

"No, they wouldn't do that," Teddy decided, after thinking it over awhile.

"They'd be afraid to stay so near Uncle Frank's ranch. Anyhow the cave isn't big enough."

"It was big enough for Clipclap."

"Yes, but he's a little pony. Anyhow, we'll look in the cave and then we'll ride on along the trail until we catch up to daddy and Uncle Frank."

"What'll they say?"

"I guess they'll be s'prised."

"Maybe they'll make us go back."

"Well, if they do we'll have some fun, anyhow," said Teddy, laughing. "Gid-dap, Clipclap."

"It's a good thing we've two ponies instead of one goat," remarked Janet, after they had ridden on a little farther.

"Course it is," agreed Ted. "We couldn't both ride Nicknack, though he could pull us both in the wagon."

"Maybe he'd be afraid of Indians," suggested Janet.

"No, I don't guess he would," answered Teddy, after some reflection. "Nicknack's a brave goat. I like him. But I like Clipclap, too."

"And I like Star Face," added Janet "He's an awful nice pony."

On and on the ponies trotted, carrying the Curlytops farther and farther from the Ring Rosy Ranch house. But the children were not afraid. The sun was shining brightly, and they had often before ridden this far alone. They could look back at the ranch buildings when they got on top of the little hills with which the prairie was dotted, and they were not lonesome.

Off on either side they could see groups of horses or cattle that belonged to Uncle Frank, and Ted and Janet thought there must be cowboys with the herds.

"I'm going to get a drink when we get to the rocks," said Janet, as they came within sight of the pile of big stones.

"Yes. And we'll give the ponies some, too," agreed her brother. "I guess they're thirsty."

Indeed the little animals were thirsty, and after they had rested a while — for Uncle Frank had told the children it was not wise to let a horse or pony drink when it was too warm — Clipclap and Star Face had some of the cool water that bubbled up among the rocks.

"It tastes awful good!" exclaimed Janet, as she took some from the cup Ted filled for her.

After Clipclap had been found at the spring, the time he was hidden in the cave, one of the cowboys had brought a tin cup to the spring, leaving it there, so if anyone passed the spring it would be easy to get a drink without having to use a hat or kneel down on the ground. For horses and cattle there was a little rocky basin into which the cool water flowed.

"I wish we could take some of the water with us," said Teddy, when, after a rest, they were ready to follow the trail again.

"If we had a bottle, like some of the cowboys carry, we could," remarked Janet. "Maybe we'll get awful thirsty if we ride on a long way, Ted."

"Maybe we will, but maybe we can find another spring. I heard Uncle Frank say there's more than one on the ranch. Come on!"

The children took another drink, and offered some to the ponies, each of which took a little. Then, once more, the Curlytops were on the trail after the Indians, as they believed.

"Which way do we go now?" asked Janet, as she watched Teddy get up in his saddle after he had helped her mount Star Face.

"We've got to follow the trail," Teddy answered.

"How do we do it?" his sister inquired.

"Well. I asked Baldy and he said just look on the ground for tracks in the dirt. You know the kind of marks a horse's foot makes, don't you, Jan?"

"Yes, and I see some down here," and she pointed to the ground.

"That's them!" exclaimed Teddy. "We've got to follow the marks! That's the trail!"

"Is this the Indians' trail?" asked the little girl, and she looked over her shoulder, perhaps to make sure no one was following her and her brother.

"I don't know if it's the Indians' trail, or, maybe, the marks left by Uncle Frank and daddy," said Teddy. "Anyhow we've got to follow the trail. That's what Baldy said."

"He doesn't know we came off alone, does he?" asked Janet

"No. I guess he wouldn't have let us if he did. But we won't have to go very far, and then we'll catch up to the rest. Then they'll have to take us with 'em."

"Yes," said Janet, and she rode along beside her brother.

Neither of the Curlytops stopped to think that their father, Uncle Frank and the cowboys had started off early that morning, and must have ridden on many miles ahead. The cowboys' horses, too, could go faster than the ponies Star Pace and Clipclap, for the larger horses had longer legs.

All Teddy and Janet thought of was hurrying along as fast as they could go, in order to catch up to the Indian hunters. What would happen after that they did not know.

All at once, as the Curlytops were riding along, they heard what they thought was a whistle.

"Some one is calling us," said Janet, turning to look back. "Did you hear that, Ted?"

"Yes, I heard a whistle. Maybe it's Uncle Frank, or some of the cowboys."

The children looked across the prairie but could see no one. They were about to go on again when the whistle sounded once more.

"That is some one calling us," declared Jan. "Let's see if we can't find who it is, Teddy."

So the children looked around again, but no one was in sight, and, what was still stranger, the whistling sound kept up.

"It's some one playing a joke on us, and hiding after they whistle," said Janet. "Maybe one of the cowboys from the ranch."

"Maybe an Indian," said Ted, and then he was sorry he had said that, for his sister looked frightened.

"Oh!" said Janet, "if it's an Indian —"

"I don't guess it is," Teddy hastened to say. "I guess Indians don't whistle, anyhow."

This made Janet feel better and once more she and her brother looked around to see what made the queer whistling sound, that still kept up. It was just like a boy calling to another, and Teddy was quite puzzled over it until he suddenly saw what was doing it.

Perched on a small mound of earth near a hole in the ground, was a little animal, about as big as a large rat, though, as Janet said, he was "nicer looking." And as Ted and his sister looked, they saw this little animal move, and then they knew he it was that was whistling.

"Oh, what is it?" cried Janet.

"I know," Teddy answered. "That's a prairie dog. Baldy told me about them, and how they whistled when they saw any danger."

"Is there any danger here?" asked Janet, looking around.

"I guess the prairie dog thinks we're the danger," said Teddy. "But we wouldn't hurt him."

"Does he live down in that hole?" asked Janet.

"Yes, just like a gopher," answered her brother, who had listened to the cowboys telling about the little prairie dogs. "And sometimes there are snakes or an owl in the same hole with the prairie dog."

"Then I'm not going any nearer," decided Janet. "I don't mind an owl, but I don't like snakes! Come on, Ted, let's hurry."

As they started off, the prairie dog, which really did make a whistling sound, suddenly darted down inside his burrow or hole. Perhaps he thought Teddy and Janet were coming to carry him off, but they were not. The children saw many more of the little animals as they rode over the prairies.

"But we must look for marks—tracks, Baldy calls them," said Teddy. "Tracks will tell us which way the Indians went," and so the children kept their eyes turned toward the sod as they rode along.

For a while they could see many marks in the soft ground—the marks of horses' feet, some shod with iron shoes and others bare, for on the prairie grass there is not the same need of iron shoes on the hoofs of horses as in the city, with its hard, paved streets. Then the marks were not so plain; and pretty soon, about a mile from the spring amid the rocks where the ground was quite hard, Teddy and Janet could see no marks at all.

"Which way do we go?" asked Ted's sister, as he called to his pony to stop. "Do you know the way?"

"No, I don't guess I do," he answered. "But anyhow we can ride along and maybe well see 'em."

"Yes, we can do that," Janet said.

It was still early in the afternoon, and the sun was shining brightly. They knew they were still on Uncle Frank's ranch, and, though they could not see the buildings any more, they could see the place where they had had a drink at the spring.

"All we've got to do, if we want to come back," observed Teddy, "is ride to the rocks and then we know the way home from there."

"Yes, that's easy," Janet said.

So they rode on and on.

Of course the Curlytops ought not to have done what they did, but they did not think, any more than Trouble thought when he opened the corral gate and let out the ponies.

But the sun did not stay high in the sky all the afternoon. Presently the bright ball of fire began to go down in the west, and the shadows of Teddy and Janet grew long on the prairie. They knew what those long shadows meant — that it was getting late afternoon.

After a while Janet turned in her saddle and looked back.

"Oh, Teddy!" she cried. "I can't see the spring rocks," for that is what the children had called the place where they had found Clipclap.

"They're back there just the same."

"I know. But if we can't see 'em we won't know how to ride back to them," went on Janet. "How are we going to find our way back home, Ted?"

"Oh, I can get to the rocks when I want to," he said. "Come on, we'll ride a little bit farther and then, if we can't find daddy and Uncle Frank, we'll go back."

"Well, don't go much farther," said Janet, and Teddy said he would not.

There were many hills and hollows now, much higher and deeper ones than those near the ranch buildings. Even from the top of one of the high hills up which the ponies slowly climbed, the Curlytops could not see the spring rocks.

"Oh, Ted!" exclaimed Jan, "I'm afraid! I want to go back! It's going to be night pretty soon!"

"It won't be night for a good while," he said, "but I guess maybe we'd better go back. I can't see daddy, Uncle Frank or the cowboys."

He raised himself in the stirrups and looked across the prairies, shading his eyes with his hand the way he had seen some of the cowboys do. Nothing was in sight.

"Come on, Jan, we'll go back," he said.

Clipclap and Star Face were turned around. Once more off trotted the little ponies with the Curlytops on their backs.

The shadows grew longer. It was not so bright and nice on the prairies now. Janet kept close to Teddy. At last she asked:

"Do you see the rocks?"

"Not yet," her brother answered. "But we'll soon be there."

They did not reach them, however. On and on they rode. The sun went down behind a bank of clouds.

"Oh, dear!" sighed Janet, "I don't like this," and her voice sounded as if she were going to cry.

"We'll soon be back at the rocks, and then I know the way home," said Teddy, as bravely as he could.

But they did not reach the rocks. Up the hollows and across the hills they rode, over the broad prairies, but no rocks did they see. At last the ponies began to go more slowly, for they were tired. It grew darker. Ted looked anxiously about. Janet spoke softly to him.

"Teddy," she asked, "are we—are we—lost?"

For a moment Teddy did not answer. Then he replied slowly:

"Yes—I guess we are lost, Janet!"

CHAPTER XIX

THE HIDDEN VALLEY

The Curlytops were in trouble. It was not the first time they had been lost, no indeed! But it was the first time they could remember being lost so far away from home, and in such a big place as a Western prairie. They did not know what to do.

"Don't you know the way home?" asked Janet, still keeping close to her brother. It was getting dark, and, somehow, she felt safer near him, even if he was only a year older than she was.

"I'd know the way home back to the ranch house if we could find the rocks with the cave where Clipclap was," Teddy replied.

"Let's look for them some more," suggested Janet. "If we don't get home pretty soon we'll be all in the dark and—and we'll have to stay out here all alone."

"Are you afraid?" asked Ted, looking at his sister.

"Yes. Won't you be?"

"Pooh! No!" he exclaimed, and he talked loudly, perhaps just so he would not be afraid. You know a boy always whistles very loudly at night when he is walking along a dark place alone. And if there are two boys they both whistle. What girls do when they walk through a dark place alone I do not know. Maybe they sing.

Anyhow Teddy talked very loud, and when Janet heard him say he was not afraid she felt better.

"But will we have to stay out here all night?" she asked.

"I guess so." Teddy answered. "But it'll be just like camping out. Daddy and Uncle Frank and the cowboys are going to stay out."

"Yes, but they've got something to eat," objected Janet, "and we haven't anything. Not even a cookie—lessen you've got one in your pocket, Teddy."

"No, Jan," answered her brother, after a quick search, "I haven't. I forgot to bring any."

"So did I," went on Janet. "I don't think I like to stay out here alone all night if we haven't anything to eat."

"No, it won't be much fun," agreed Teddy. "I guess maybe I can find those rocks, Janet, and then we'll know how to get home. Come on."

He turned his pony's head and the tired little animal walked slowly on and Janet's Star Face followed. But the truth of the matter was, Ted did not know in which direction to guide his little horse. He could not remember where the rocks lay. But Janet was trusting to him, and he felt he must do his best.

So he kept on until it grew a little darker, and his pony was walking so slowly that Trouble would have found it easy to have walked almost as fast.

"What's the matter?" asked Janet, who was riding behind her brother, looking as hard as she could through the darkness for a sight of the rocks, which, once they were reached, almost meant home. "What's the matter, Ted?"

"Matter with what, Jan?"

"What makes the ponies go so slow?"

"'Cause they're tired, I guess."

"Can't you find the rocks and let them rest and get a drink? I'm awful thirsty, Teddy!"

"So'm I, Jan. We'll go on a little more and maybe we'll find the rocks. Don't cry!"

"Pooh! who's goin' to cry?" demanded Janet quickly.

"I—I thought maybe you were," Teddy answered.

"I am not!" and Janet was very positive about it. "But I'm tired and hungry, and I want a drink awful bad."

"So do I," added Teddy. "We'll go on a little more."

So, wearily, the ponies walked on carrying the Curlytops. Ted kept looking ahead, and to the left and right, trying to find the rocks. But, had he only known it (which he did later) he was going away from them all the while instead of toward them.

All at once Clipclap stumbled and nearly fell.

"Whoa there! Look out!" cried Teddy, reining up the head of his animal as he had seen Uncle Frank do. "Don't fall, Clipclap!"

"What's the matter?" asked Janet. "Did he step in a hole?"

"I don't know. I guess he's just tired," and Teddy's voice was sad. For he was very weary and much frightened, though he did not tell Janet so.

"Well, let's stop and rest," said his sister. "Do you think you can find those rocks, Ted?"

"No, I don't guess I can. I guess we're lost, Janet."

"Oh, dear!" she answered.

"Now don't cry!" warned Teddy.

"I—I'm not!" exclaimed his sister. "I—I was just blowing my nose, so there, The-o-dore Mar-tin!"

Teddy grinned in the darkness, tired as he was. He was glad Janet was a little angry with him. That meant she would not cry, and if his sister started to weep Ted did not know what he would do. He might even cry himself. He was not too big for that.

"Let's stop and give the ponies a rest," suggested Janet.

"All right," agreed Teddy. "And maybe they can hunt around and find water. One of the cowboys told me his pony did that once when he didn't know where to get a drink himself."

"I wish Star Face could find water," went on Janet. "I'd drink some of it, too."

"So would I—if it was clean," said Teddy.

Wearily the two Curlytops slipped from their saddles. The ponies seemed glad of this, and at once began to eat the grass that grew all about. Teddy and Janet looked at them awhile. It was not so dark but what they could see things close to them, and the stars were twinkling brightly overhead.

"They don't seem very thirsty," said Janet.

"Maybe they'll start to go after water when they've had their supper," suggested her brother, with a sigh, which, however, Janet did not hear. "We've got to wait—that's all."

The Curlytops sat down on the ground and waited, while the ponies with the reins over their heads—which was a sign that they must not go far away—cropped the sweet grass.

"I wish we could eat grass," said Janet, after a bit.

"Why?"

"Then we could eat it like the ponies do and not be hungry."

"It would be a good thing," Teddy agreed. "But we can't. I chewed some sour grass once, but I didn't swallow it."

"I ate some watercress once at home," said Janet. "But I didn't like it. Anyhow I don't guess watercress grows around here."

"No," agreed Teddy.

Then they sat and watched the ponies eating in the darkness. Clipclap was wandering farther off than Teddy liked and he jumped up and hurried after his animal. As he caught him Teddy saw something on the ground a little way off. It was something round and black, and, now that the moon had come up, he could see more plainly.

"What's the matter, Teddy?" Janet called to him, as she saw him standing motionless, after he had taken hold of Clipclap's bridle. "What are you looking at?"

"I don't know what it is," Teddy answered. "Maybe it's a prairie dog, but he's keepin' awful still. Come and look, Janet."

"Oh, I don't want to!" she exclaimed.

135

"Oh, come on!" urged Teddy. "It isn't moving. Maybe you can tell what it is."

Janet, making sure that Star Face was all right, walked over to her brother. She, too, saw the dark object lying on a bare spot in the prairie. It did not move. The moonlight became stronger and Janet, becoming brave all of a sudden, went closer.

"It's nothing but a bundle, Teddy Martin!" she exclaimed. "Somebody has dropped a bundle."

"They have?" Teddy cried. "Then if somebody's been past here they can find us — or we can find them — and we aren't lost anymore!"

"Oh, I hope it comes true!" sighed Janet.

"Here, you hold Clipclap — he's starting to walk away" — went on Teddy, "and I'll go see what that is."

Janet took the pony's reins, and her brother walked toward the bundle. He could see now that it was something wrapped in a blanket, and as he came closer he saw that the blanket was one of the kind the cowboys at Uncle Frank's ranch carried when they went out to spend the night on the prairie.

"What is it?" asked Janet, as her brother picked up the bundle and came back toward her.

"I don't know, but it's heavy," he answered. "Well open it."

"Maybe we'd better not," cautioned Janet. "It isn't ours."

"But we're lost," Teddy said, "and we want to be found. Maybe there's something in this bundle to help."

The blanket was fastened with a strap on the outside, and Teddy managed to unbuckle this after two or three trials, Janet helping. Then, as the moon shone down on what was in the blanket, the Curlytops gave a cry of delight, which startled even the ponies.

"It's something to eat!" cried Teddy.

"And to drink!" added Janet, as she picked up the canvas-covered canteen, or water bottle, such as soldiers carry. By shaking it she knew it was full of water.

"Say, this is good luck!" cried Teddy.

Stopping no longer to wonder who had dropped the bundle, the Curlytops took a drink from the canteen. They had not been used to drinking out of a bottle since they were babies, and some of the water ran down their necks.

But they did not mind this. And, even though the water was rather warm, they felt much better after having had a drink.

"I wish we could give the ponies some," said Janet. "But there isn't very much, and they would drink this all up and not know they'd had any."

"Anyhow I guess they're not thirsty, or they'd try to find water just as the cowboys said they would," added Teddy. "They can chew the grass."

He and Janet looked into the bundle again, and found a number of sandwiches, together with some uncooked bacon, a little ground coffee, a small coffee-pot and a tin cup.

"Oh, goody! We can eat the sandwiches," Janet said.

"And in the morning, when we find a spring, we can make coffee," added Teddy. "I know how, 'cause grandpa showed me when we were camping on Star Island. I haven't any matches to make a fire, but maybe I can find some."

"Will we have to stay here all night?" asked Janet anxiously.

"I spect so," her brother answered. "I don't know the way back to the ranch house. We can't even find the rocks. We'll stay here all night. It isn't cold, and now we have a blanket we can wrap up in it like the cowboys do. And we've something to eat and drink."

"But mother and daddy will be awful worried," said Janet.

"Well, they'll maybe come and find us," answered Teddy. "Look out!" he cried. "Clipclap's going off again!"

Indeed the little pony seemed to want to walk away, and so did Star Face.

"Maybe they know where to go to find water," suggested Janet.

"Maybe," agreed Ted. "Let's let 'em go, and we'll go with 'em. That water in the canteen won't be enough till morning."

The children ate nearly all of the sandwiches, and put away the rest of the food in the blanket which Teddy strapped around it. Then they mounted their ponies, Ted taking the bundle with him, and let the animals wander which way they would.

"They'll go to water if they're thirsty enough," Teddy said.

"Who do you s'pose dropped that bundle?" asked Janet.

"A cowboy," her brother answered.

"One from Ring Rosy Ranch?"

"Maybe."

"Oh, I hope he did, and that he's around here somewhere," went on Janet. "I'm tired of being lost!"

"We've only just begun," Teddy said. But, truth to tell, he wished very much that they were both safe back at the ranch house with their mother.

On and on over the moonlit prairies went Star Face and Clipclap. They seemed to know where they were going and did not stop. Ted and Janet were too tired to guide them. They were both getting sleepy.

Pretty soon Janet saw ahead of her something glistening in the stretch of the prairie. The moonlight seemed to sparkle on it.

"Oh, look, Ted!" she cried, pointing.

"It's water—a little river!" he exclaimed. "The ponies have led us to water!"

And so the animals had. Teddy and Janet slipped from their ponies' backs at the edge of the stream and then Star Face and Clipclap took long drinks. Ted emptied the canteen, filled it with the cooler water, and he and Janet drank again. Then they felt much better.

The ponies again began to crop the grass. The Curlytops, very tired and sleepy, felt that it would be all right to make their bed in the blanket they had found, dropped by some passing cowboy.

But first Ted looked around. Off to one side, and along the stream from which they had drunk, he saw something dark looming up.

"Look, Janet," he said. "Maybe that's a ranch house over there, and we could go in for the night."

"Maybe," she agreed. "Let's go to it."

Once more they mounted their ponies. The animals did not seem so tired now, but trotted on over the prairie. They drew nearer to the dark blotch Teddy had noticed.

Then, as the moon came out from behind some clouds, the Curlytops saw that they were at the entrance to a hidden valley—a little valley tucked away among the hills, which they would never have seen had they not come to the stream to drink.

The little river ran through the valley, and in the moonlight the children could see that a fence had been made at the end nearest them. It was a wooden fence, and not one of barbed wire, such as there were many of on Ring Rosy Ranch.

"This is a queer valley," said Janet.

"Yes, and look!" exclaimed Ted, pointing. "Don't you see things moving around in it?"

"Yes," agreed Jan, as she looked. "Why, Ted!" she cried. "They're horses— ponies—a lot of 'em!"

"So they are!" exclaimed Ted. "Oh, we're near a ranch, Janet! Now we're all right!"

"Yes. But maybe we're a good way from the ranch house," answered Janet. "We maybe can't find it in the dark. Some of Uncle Frank's ponies are five miles away from the stable, you know. Maybe we'd better not go on any more in the dark. I'm tired!"

"Well," agreed Teddy. "I guess we could stay here till it's morning. We could sleep in the blanket. It's plenty big enough for us two."

"And in the morning we can ride on and find the ranch, and the cowboys there will take us to Ring Rosy," added Janet. "Let's do it, Teddy."

They looked again at the strange valley in which the horses were moving about. Clipclap whinnied and one of the other ponies answered. But they could not come out because of the fence, part of which was built in and across the little river.

Then, throwing the reins over the heads f their ponies, and knowing the animals would not stray far, Ted and Janet, taking another drink from the canteen, rolled up in the blanket and went to sleep on the prairie just outside the hidden valley that held a secret of which they did not even dream.

CHAPTER XX
BACK TO RING ROSY

"I hope the Curlytops won't ride too far," said Mrs. Martin, coming out into the kitchen to help with the work.

She had just got Trouble to sleep after Teddy and Janet had brought him in from the haymow before riding off on their ponies.

"Oh, I guess they won't," Aunt Millie answered.

But, could Mrs. Martin and Aunt Millie have seen them, they would have been much surprised to know where the Curlytops then were.

As you know, they were riding along the trail after the Indians.

The hours went on until it was late afternoon. And then, when the children did not come back, Mrs. Martin began to be alarmed. She went to the top of a low hill not far away from the ranch house and looked across the prairie.

"I can't see them," she said, when she came back.

"Oh, don't worry," returned Aunt Millie. "They'll be along pretty soon. And, anyhow, there is no danger."

"But—the Indians?" questioned Mrs. Martin.

"Oh, they are far enough off by this time," said the ranch owner's wife. "They won't bother the Curly tops."

But Mother Martin did worry, and when supper time came near and Janet and Teddy were not yet back, Aunt Millie, too, began to think it strange.

"What do you suppose could happen?" asked Mrs. Martin. "I wish Dick were here."

"Oh, lots of little things might happen," said Aunt Millie. "The children may have ridden farther than they meant to. It's such a nice day for riding you couldn't blame them for going. Or one of their ponies may have gone lame and have to walk slowly. That would make them get here late."

"Suppose they should be hurt?" asked Mother Martin, anxiously.

"Oh, I don't suppose anything of the sort!" and Aunt Millie laughed. But Mother Martin did not feel like laughing.

At last, however, when it began to get dark and the children had not come, even the cowboys left at the ranch — those who had not ridden on the trail after the Indians — said it was time something was done.

"We'll go out and find 'em," said Baldy. "The little tykes have got lost; that's about all. We'll find 'em and bring 'em home!"

"Oh, I hope you can!" exclaimed Mrs. Martin.

"Sure we will!" cried Baldy. "Won't we, boys?"

"That's what we will!" cried the cowboys.

The men started out over the prairie right after supper, carrying lanterns, not so much that they needed the lights as that they might be seen by the lost children.

"Hello, Curlytops! where are you?" called the cowboys.

But no one answered them. Teddy and Janet were far away.

The cowboys rode as far as the pile of rocks where the spring bubbled up. There Baldy, swinging his lantern to and fro, said he thought he could see the marks of the feet of Star Face and Clipclap among those of other ponies, but he was not sure.

"We'll have to come back here and start out early in the morning when we can see better," he said.

"And what are we going to do all night?" asked another cowboy.

"Well, we'll keep on hunting, of course. But I don't believe well find the lost Curlytops."

One of the men rode back to the ranch to tell Mrs. Martin that so far, no trace of the missing children had been found. She could not keep back her tears, but she tried to be brave.

"Oh, where can they be?" she asked.

"They'll be all right," the cowboy said. "It's a nice warm night, and they're brave children. Even if they had to sleep out it would not hurt 'em. They could take the blankets that are under the ponies' saddles and wrap up in them. They'll be all right."

Though they were lost, the Curlytops were, at that moment, much better off than the cowboy thought. For they had found the big blanket and the bundle of food, and they were sleeping soundly on the prairie.

At first they had been a little afraid to lie down all alone out in the night, but their ponies were with them, and Janet said it felt as though Clipclap and Star Face were like good watch dogs.

Then, being very tired and having had something to eat and drink, they fell asleep.

All night long, though, the cowboys rode over the prairie looking for the lost ones. They shouted and called, but the Curlytops were too far away to hear or to answer, even if they had been awake.

"Well, now we can make a better hunt," said Baldy, when he saw the sun beginning to rise. "We'll get something to eat and start out from the spring in the rocks. I'm almost sure the Curlytops were there."

Mrs. Martin had not slept all night, and when the cowboys came back to breakfast she said she was going to ride with them to search for her children.

"Yes, I think it would do you good," said Aunt Millie.

Mrs. Martin had learned how to ride when a girl, and she had practised some since coming to Ring Rosy Ranch. So she did not feel strange in the saddle. With Baldy and the other cowboys she set off.

They went to the spring amid the rocks and there began the search. Over the prairie the riders spread out like a big fan, looking everywhere for the lost ones. And when they were not found in about an hour Baldy said:

"Well, there's just a chance that their ponies took them to Silver Creek."

"Where's that?" asked Mrs. Martin.

"It's a stream of water quite a way off," Baldy answered. "It isn't on our ranch, and we don't very often go there. But if the Curlytops' ponies were thirsty in the night they might go to Silver Creek, even if Jan and Ted didn't want them to. I think the ponies went the nearest way to water."

"Then let us go that way!" cried Mrs. Martin.

Meanwhile Teddy and Janet had awakened. They could look right into the strange valley through which flowed Silver Creek, though they did not then know its name.

"And look what a lot of horses!" cried Janet.

"And cows!" added her brother. "I wonder whose they are?"

"Oh, I guess they live on some ranch," Janet said. "Now if we can find the ranch house we'll be all right."

"We'll look for it," suggested Teddy. "But first we've got to have breakfast. If I had a match I could make a fire and boil some coffee."

"Let's not bother with breakfast," suggested Janet. "I'm not very hungry. And if we find the ranch house we can get something to eat there. Come on, Teddy."

They got a drink at the stream, and then, rolling up what food was left in the blanket, they got on their ponies and rode away, going around the valley instead of into it, for Teddy saw that hills closed it at the far end.

"There's no ranch house in that valley," he said.

The Curlytops had not ridden far before Janet, who had gone a little ahead of Teddy, cried:

"Oh, look! Here come some cowboys!"

"I guess they belong to this ranch — the one where we saw the ponies and cows," replied Teddy, as he saw a number of horsemen riding toward them. The horsemen began to whoop and shout, and their horses ran very fast toward the Curlytops.

"There's a lady with 'em," remarked Janet.

"They seem awful glad to meet us," went on Teddy. "Look, they're wavin' their hats."

And so the cowboys were. When the riders came a little nearer Teddy and Janet rubbed their eyes in surprise.

"Why — why!" Teddy exclaimed. "There's our own Baldy!"

"And there's mother!" fairly shouted Janet. "Oh, Mother! Mother!" she cried. "Oh, how glad I am!" and she made Star Face run toward the lady on horseback.

"Oh, my dear children! Where have you been?" asked Mrs. Martin, a little later, as she hugged first Janet and then Teddy.

"We — we got lost," Teddy answered.

"Yes, but you ran away, and that was not right," his mother told him. "Where did you go?"

"We — we went on the trail after the Indians," Teddy answered.

"Did you find them?" asked Baldy with a smile.

"No, but we found a lot of horses and cows back there in a little valley with a fence," said Janet. "And we were going to ride to the ranch house when we saw you."

"Ranch house!" cried Baldy. "There isn't a ranch house within fifteen miles except the one at Ring Rosy. Did you say you saw some cows and horses!"

"Yes. In a valley," explained Teddy.

"Show us where it was!" eagerly cried the cowboy, and when the Curlytops had ridden to it, with Baldy and the others following, the lame cowboy, whose foot was a little better, exclaimed:

"Well, if the Curlytops haven't gone and done it!"

"Done what?" asked their mother.

"They've found the lost cattle and horses!"

"You mean Uncle Frank's!" asked Teddy.

"That's just what I mean! These are the horses and cattle the Indians drove away. The Redmen put the animals in this valley and made a fence at this end so they couldn't get out. They knew the horses and cattle would have water to drink and grass to eat, and they'd stay here a long while — until the Indians would have a chance to drive 'em farther away and sell 'em."

"Yes, that's just what they did. I never thought of this valley, though I saw it quite a few years ago. I've never been here since. The Indians knew it would be a good place to hide the horses they stole, and we might never have found 'em if it hadn't been for you Curlytops."

"I'm glad!" said Teddy.

"So'm I," said Janet, "and I'm hungry, too!"

"Well, well soon have you back at Ring Rosy Ranch, where there's a good breakfast!" laughed Baldy. "Well! Well! To think of you Curlytops finding what we cowboys were looking all over for!"

"And are daddy and Uncle Frank looking for these horses and cattle?" asked Teddy.

"Yes. And for the Indians that took 'em. But I guess they won't find either," Baldy answered.

And Baldy was right. Some hours after the Curlytops were back at Ring Rosy Ranch, in rode Uncle Frank and the others. They had not found what they had gone after, and you can imagine how surprised they all were when told that Ted and Janet had, by accident, found the lost cattle and horses in the hidden valley.

"You're regular cowboys!" cried Uncle Frank.

"I knew they'd turn out all right when they learned to ride ponyback!" said Daddy Martin. "Though you mustn't ride on the trail alone after Indians again!" he said.

Teddy and Janet told all that had happened to them, from getting lost, to finding the blanket and going to sleep in it on the open prairie.

One of the cowboys with Uncle Frank had lost the blanket, and he said he was glad he dropped it, since it gave Teddy and Janet something to eat and something to wrap up in.

That afternoon the stolen horses and cattle were driven in from the hidden valley; so the Indians did not get them after all. And a little later some soldiers came to keep guard over the Redmen so they could not again go off their reservation to make trouble. All of Uncle Frank's animals, except a few that the Indians had sold, were found, and the Curlytops were the pride of Ring Rosy Ranch as long as they remained there.

"Well, I wonder if we'll have any more adventures," said Janet to her brother one day, about a week after they were lost and had been found.

"Oh, I guess so," he answered. "Anyhow, we've got two nice ponies, and we can have lots of rides. Come on, I'll race you."

The bright summer days brought more fun to Teddy and Janet at Uncle Frank's ranch. They rode many miles on Star Face and Clipclap, sometimes taking Trouble with them.

"I want to dwive," said the little fellow one day, as he sat on the saddle in front of his brother.

"All right, you may drive a little while," Teddy answered, and he let Baby William hold the reins.

"Now I a cowboy!" exclaimed the little fellow. "Gid-dap, Clipclap! I go lasso a Injun!"

Ted and Janet laughed at this.

And so, leaving the Curlytops to their fun, we will say good-bye.

THE END

Milton Keynes UK
Ingram Content Group UK Ltd.
UKHW010703260923
429409UK00004B/362